'I asked the wrong
didn't I? I a
Toby was bor
our night toge

Brooke swallowed h

'But he wasn't bor... ...months after our night together, was he?' His blue eyes glittered dangerously and his tone was acid. 'He was born *seven* months afterwards. I thought you were evasive because you were concealing your relationship with another man, not because you were hiding the fact that we made a child together. So if I'd asked the question a different way, would you have told me the truth? Would you?'

'Jed, please—'

'The truth, Brooke.' Jed's eyes were now cold and unsympathetic. 'I want it now. Straight and with no omissions.'

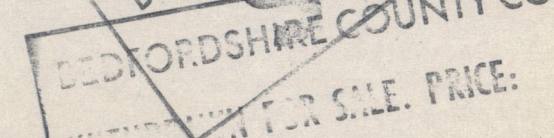

Sarah Morgan trained as a nurse and has since worked in a variety of health-related jobs. Married to a gorgeous businessman who still makes her knees knock, she spends most of her time trying to keep up with their two little boys but manages to sneak off occasionally to indulge her passion for writing romance. Sarah loves outdoor life and is an enthusiastic skier and walker. Whatever she is doing, her head is always full of new characters and she is addicted to happy endings.

Recent titles by the same author:

WORTH THE RISK

THE MIDWIFE'S CHILD

BY
SARAH MORGAN

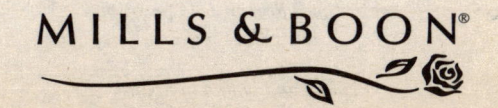

MILLS & BOON

DID YOU PURCHASE THIS BOOK WITHOUT A COVER?
If you did, you should be aware it is **stolen property** as it was reported *unsold and destroyed* by a retailer. Neither the author nor the publisher has received any payment for this book.

All the characters in this book have no existence outside the imagination of the author, and have no relation whatsoever to anyone bearing the same name or names. They are not even distantly inspired by any individual known or unknown to the author, and all the incidents are pure invention.

All Rights Reserved including the right of reproduction in whole or in part in any form. This edition is published by arrangement with Harlequin Enterprises II B.V. The text of this publication or any part thereof may not be reproduced or transmitted in any form or by any means, electronic or mechanical, including photocopying, recording, storage in an information retrieval system, or otherwise, without the written permission of the publisher.

This book is sold subject to the condition that it shall not, by way of trade or otherwise, be lent, resold, hired out or otherwise circulated without the prior consent of the publisher in any form of binding or cover other than that in which it is published and without a similar condition including this condition being imposed on the subsequent purchaser.

MILLS & BOON and MILLS & BOON with the Rose Device are registered trademarks of the publisher.

First published in Great Britain 2001
Harlequin Mills & Boon Limited,
Eton House, 18-24 Paradise Road, Richmond, Surrey TW9 1SR

© Sarah Morgan 2001

ISBN 0 263 82659 7

Set in Times Roman 10½ on 11 pt.
03-0401-53926

Printed and bound in Spain
by Litografia Rosés, S.A., Barcelona

PROLOGUE

'*WHAT DO YOU MEAN, you can't find her?*'

Jed paced the floor angrily, his hands thrust into the pockets of his white coat as he glowered at his brother. 'Think, man! It's your hospital, for goodness' sake. You trained there, you know everyone. You must know who she is. Concentrate!'

'It's not concentration I need, it's information,' Tom pointed out mildly. 'Jed, be reasonable. What have you given me to go on? All you can say is that you don't think she's a doctor. No name, no age, no nothing! You don't even know she works in my hospital!'

'Of course she works in your hospital.' Jed stopped pacing and frowned impatiently. 'Why else would she have been at the Christmas Ball?'

'She could have been someone's guest. Did you think of that? You were my guest, remember? You don't work there...' Tom watched his brother's face and then shook his head slowly. 'How on earth did you get the highest marks ever recorded at your medical school? For someone of supposed exceptional intelligence, you're being remarkably slow in your thinking.'

'She wasn't anyone's guest.' Jed stared out of the ward office window to the bustling London street twenty-eight floors below.

'How do you know?'

Jed shrugged and shook his head slowly. 'Something she said...'

'Oh, you did manage some sort of conversation, then.' Tom's lazy drawl was loaded with sarcasm and Jed turned, his handsome face set as he glared at his brother.

'This is a joke to you, isn't it?'

'Well, no, not a joke exactly.' Tom shifted uncomfortably under his brother's penetrating stare. 'But even you have to appreciate the irony of the situation.'

Jed gritted his teeth and his eyes narrowed. 'I do?'

'Oh, come on, Jed!' Tom leaned back in his chair and risked a grin. 'All your life you've had women tripping over each other to get to you. Now, at last, we discover that there is, in fact, at least one woman in the world who can resist your charms. It gives the rest of us poor mortals some hope. Maybe she doesn't go for the tough, macho sort. You could loosen up a little, you know—'

'Unless you want to find out just how macho and tough I can be, you should give it a rest,' his brother said dryly, turning back to stare out of the window. 'I thought you knew everyone in this hospital.'

'I know everyone worth knowing,' Tom agreed, helping himself to the last biscuit from a packet abandoned on the low coffee-table. 'And, believe me, your mystery woman doesn't work here.'

Jed made an impatient sound. 'You don't know—'

'Hear me out, will you?' Tom lobbed the empty biscuit packet into the bin and gave his brother an injured look. 'I've made discreet enquiries and turned up nothing, but that's hardly surprising, considering the dearth of information you gave me to go on. I tell you this, if I ever give up medicine I will not be setting up as a private detective.'

He rummaged in his pocket and retrieved a crumpled piece of paper. 'Here we are. This was the doctors' ball, remember, and according to my sources there were only eight tickets sold to non-medical staff—the tickets were like gold dust. Because I'm the best brother in the world and I'm intrigued to see you seriously smitten for the first time in your life, I've tracked down each one of those eight individuals and had a good look at them. Three of them were blonde and three of them had short hair so that rules them out. No way did they match the description of your girl.'

Jed was watching him intently. 'What about the other two?'

'Don't get your hopes up.' His brother shook his head dolefully. 'One of them is Annie Foster, that gorgeous sister on ITU who I went out with for two months, so we know it's not her. And the last one doesn't even remotely match the description you gave me, so unless you were seeing her through rose-tinted glasses your girl doesn't exist.'

Jed stiffened and a muscle worked in his jaw, 'She definitely exists and you know I don't wear glasses, rose-tinted or otherwise.'

'Well, there's your answer!' Tom grinned cheekily and tossed the paper at his brother. 'You're eyesight's going and you couldn't see her properly. She probably wasn't "dark and stunning with legs like a gazelle" at all, she was dumpy, mousy and plain. So she could be number eight.'

Jed leaned broad shoulders against the wall, his tone deceptively mild. 'Have I ever warned you that your sense of humour is life-threatening?'

'My life or yours?' Tom caught the look in his brother's eye and subsided rapidly. 'Sorry, sorry. Look, are you sure she wasn't a doctor?'

Jed pulled a face. 'No, I'm not sure. I'm not sure of anything at all. I just got the impression that she did something else.'

'Well, that narrows it down,' Tom drawled sarcastically. 'Nurse, cleaner, radiographer, physiotherapist—the options are truly limited. Can't you give me anything else to go on? I mean, why on earth didn't you get her name? How could you whisper sweet nothings if you didn't know her name?'

Jed turned away again, his eyes scanning the streetlights glowing far below as he remembered that night.

He'd noticed her almost straight away, leaning against one of the pillars in the ballroom, her black hair bubbling down her bare back, her eyes fixed on the people dancing. He'd watched curiously as man after man had approached her and been turned away. And then she'd moved her head and had seen him, those beautiful coal black eyes widening as they'd fixed on his, her chin lifting slightly as if daring him to approach her. Which he had, of course, partly because she'd been the most stunning woman he'd ever seen, and partly because her aloofness had represented a challenge and he'd never been able to resist a challenge.

And after that—

He sighed. 'We didn't bother with names.'

'I see.' Tom rubbed his chin to hide the smile and shook his head in disbelief. 'It must have been some night...'

Jed's shoulders tensed. It had been incredible, but he didn't expect his playboy brother to begin to understand that. Even he didn't understand the way he felt so how could he expect his brother to? 'I suppose it never occurred to me that she'd run.'

'Yeah, that must have been a first.' Tom's voice was dry and Jed turned with a frown.

'Meaning?'

Tom rolled his eyes and lounged back in his chair. 'Has anyone run from you before? No. Normally they're beating your door down. So maybe you scared her or something. Or maybe she just found you repulsive.'

'I didn't scare her.' Or maybe he had. He frowned. The intensity of feeling between them had been so overwhelming it had knocked him for six. Maybe it had frightened her, too. After all, she'd never— 'She certainly didn't find me repulsive.'

'Well, she didn't stick around for more, did she?' Tom hesitated, his dark eyes fixed on his brother. 'I hate to be the one to point out the obvious, but if she'd wanted you to find her, she would have left her number. Women don't just disappear if they want to be found. Maybe she wasn't really interested.'

There was a long silence and then Jed took a deep breath, still not looking at his brother. 'She was interested.'

'Then why did she sneak off?'

'Dammit, I don't know.' Jed thumped his fist on the glass

and closed his eyes briefly. 'I don't know. But it wasn't anything to do with us. It was something else. She was very secretive and wary—'

'She was probably married.' Tom's voice was dry but a strange look crossed Jed's handsome face and he shook his head.

'No. Definitely not that.'

Tom watched him curiously and then shrugged. 'How do you know? She might have been leading you a dance and—'

'She wasn't married.' Jed's voice was steady and his eyes glittered with a strange light. There was no way she could have been married. That was one of the few things he *did* know about her.

'Right.' Tom cleared his throat and decided not to pursue it. 'Well, if she wasn't married, maybe it just wasn't right—'

'We were perfect together, Tom.'

Tom muttered under his breath and leaned forward in his chair, urging his brother to see sense. 'One night, Jed. Get a grip, man! It was the romance of it all—the mistletoe, the Christmas-tree lights, snow on the ground. It wasn't real.'

Jed stared out into the darkness and remembered the laughter, the warmth and the passion. He remembered a girl with wild dark hair and bright sharp eyes, an intriguing mixture of fire and innocence. It had been the most amazing night of his life.

'Oh, it was real,' he murmured. 'And I'm going to find her.'

'I don't suppose she dropped a glass slipper in your flat? You could try it on all the women in the infirmary, starting with the really ugly ones...' Tom caught the look on his brother's face and lifted his hands in a gesture of surrender. 'OK, OK. I'm sorry. I was just trying to cheer you up.'

'If your wit was an indication of your brain size, your patients would be in big trouble.' Jed strode over and stood in front of him, his dark eyes gleaming with purpose. 'I've got to find her! Ask again. Ask everyone.'

'OK.' Tom frowned and shifted uncomfortably under his

brother's gaze. 'I'll do my best. Back off, will you? If you glared at her like that it's no wonder she ran off.'

'Sorry.' Jed closed his eyes briefly and raked both hands through his hair. 'I'm sorry, but I'm desperate. I won't give up, Tom.'

'So I see. OK, I'll keep asking.' He glanced at his brother, his eyes narrowed. 'She must have been one very special lady.'

'Oh, she was.' Jed's voice was soft. 'She was.'

CHAPTER ONE

SHE was in big trouble.

Glancing at her watch with a mew of panic, Brooke careered through the pelting rain across the hospital car park, dodging puddles and pedestrians as she made a dash for the sanctuary of the hospital.

Why was her life always like this? Why? Her umbrella wavered threateningly in the strong wind and she flung a breathless apology at a pedestrian who gave her a nervous look and a wide berth. Why, for once, couldn't things have gone smoothly? Just for one day, surely life could have been kind? What had she ever done to deserve the repeated obstacles that were delivered at her door?

First the heating, then the roof and now the car. What next?

Breathless and soaked, she shouldered her way through the revolving doors of the maternity unit, and the sudden warmth of the foyer made her pause and catch her breath.

Please, please, let the day improve, she pleaded to no one in particular as she took the lift to the third floor and attempted a first-aid job on her hair which fell in a damp, tangled mass halfway down her back. Twisting it firmly, she rummaged in her pocket for some pins and fastened it securely in a knot at the back of her head, hoping that it would hold until lunchtime.

In the sanctuary of the staffroom, she stripped off her wet clothes and changed into the comfortable blue cotton trousers and tunic top that everyone wore on the labour ward.

'I'm really, really sorry, folks...' Flustered and out of breath, she paused by the door of the office where everyone from the early shift was gathered. 'I had some problems.'

'You don't need to explain.' Sister Wilson's voice was full of humour and sympathy. 'We saw you getting off the bus and sprinting across the car park. I gather that joke of a contraption that you call a car failed you again.'

Brooke nodded and bit her lip. 'It's the rain, I think. It hates rain—'

'And cold and heat,' one of the midwives interrupted with a laugh. 'Face it, Brooke, it's on its last legs. You'd better ask Father Christmas for another one.'

It was only March and most of her problems were way beyond the touch of Father Christmas, Brooke thought gloomily, tucking a wayward strand of hair behind her ear.

'I'll get an earlier bus tomorrow.' Dropping into a vacant chair, she glanced at the board to see how busy they were and her eyes widened in disbelief. 'We're full again?'

'To the point of bursting.' Gill Wilson stood up, suddenly businesslike. 'And Antenatal have got two in early labour as well so we're in for a good day. Brooke, I've allocated Paula the lady in Room 2, but as she's still a student she obviously can't take full responsibility so I'd like you to supervise. The lady's name is Alison Neal and she's a thirty-year-old primip and *very* anxious. Perhaps you should have five minutes with her on your own before Paula joins you. You're normally very good with panickers.'

'Of course.' A primip—an abbreviation for primigravida, someone having their first baby—often needed more support and reassurance than a woman who'd been through it all before, and was usually in labour for much longer.

'Suzie...' Gill Wilson turned to another midwife. 'Can you run between 4 and 5 for me and supervise the students? Diane can sort out the admissions and Helen can take the lady in room one. Oh, and by the way, things are looking up here. The new consultant started yesterday and the new senior reg starts in a few weeks so at least the medical staff won't be so stretched.'

'What's the consultant like?' Brooke draped her stethoscope round her neck and straightened her tunic.

'First class.' Gill Wilson nodded with satisfaction. 'We're very lucky to have him.'

One of the midwives gave a sigh. 'Just tell us he isn't a meddler. We don't need another consultant like—'

'Now, now,' Gill interrupted briskly, a faint frown touching her forehead. 'No need to name names. He's left and it's history and, no, Jed Matthews isn't at all like that. He's an incredibly talented obstetrician who thinks that women should do it by themselves whenever they can. I dare say you'll meet him later but I think he'll support our philosophy to the hilt.'

'Well, that's one bit of good news, then.' Brooke stood up and tucked her pen and notebook into her pocket, falling into step beside her friend Suzie as they walked down the corridor.

Suzie gave her a sympathetic look. 'You OK?'

'Are you joking?' Brooke rolled her eyes. 'When was my life ever OK?'

'What's happening about the roof?'

'I've got a man coming to see it on Saturday but at the moment I'm just using a bucket and lots of hope.'

Suzie pulled a face and looked worried. 'This rain can't last for ever.'

'This is the Lake District so it can and, knowing my luck, it probably will,' Brooke said dryly as they paused outside the door of Room 2. 'But thanks for asking.'

Suzie nodded and hesitated. 'Look, if you need a loan…'

'No, thanks.' Brooke stiffened and her small chin lifted slightly. 'I'm fine.'

'Brooke, for goodness' sake!' Suzie glanced along the corridor and lowered her voice 'You're not fine at all and you know it! You're struggling like mad and it's time you let someone help you.'

'I don't need help.' Brooke's tone was frosty and Suzie looked exasperated.

'You're so stubborn, do you know that? How will you pay for the roof?'

Brooke shrugged. 'That's my problem.' One of the many. 'I'll do some agency work or something.'

'Brooke—'

'I'll handle it.' Brooke's eyes glinted with determination and, without waiting for a reply, she shouldered her way into Room 2 and beamed at the woman sitting on the bed.

'Hello, Mrs Neal. I'm Brooke Daniels, one of the midwives on the unit.' She took one look at the wide, frightened eyes of the young woman in front of her and forced her own problems to the back of her mind, knowing that she had some serious work to do.

'Could you call me Alison?' The woman looked terrified. 'It seems more...personal somehow. I hate anything medical.'

'Try not to think of this as medical,' Brooke advised gently. 'Having a baby is perfectly natural and in this unit our policy is to intervene as little as possible.'

'Is that why this room doesn't look a bit like a hospital room?' Alison glanced round at the pretty curtains and bedspread and the comfortable sofa and beanbags. 'It's more like being at home.'

'Actually, it's better than home,' her husband pointed out dryly. 'At home we haven't got a king-size bed and a rocking chair.'

Brooke smiled. 'The rooms are nice, aren't they? The whole idea was to make people feel as though they were in the comfort of their own homes but with the advantages of hospital technology on hand if needed.'

Alison was still gripping her husband's hand tightly. 'Will you be with me all day?'

'One of our student midwives, Paula, will be with you the whole time,' Brooke told her. 'I'll be popping in and out all day and I'll definitely be here when you deliver.'

'I can't bear to think about that bit.' Alison managed a weak smile and bit her lip. 'I'm terrified, I have to confess. I can't relax at all.'

Brooke settled herself on the bed. Blow protocol. What this woman needed was the personal touch.

'Well, helping you to relax is my job.' She took Alison's other hand in hers and gave it a quick squeeze. 'Did you go to any of our antenatal classes?'

'I went to the yoga class a few times but, to be honest, the roads were so bad in December and January that I stayed at home mostly.' Alison looked anxious. 'Should I have persevered? Would it have made a big difference?'

'Well, the classes do teach you certain techniques for relaxation,' Brooke told her, 'but if you went a few times then you will have grasped the basics. We use lots of different methods to help you relax here—aromatherapy, the water pool and massage for starters.'

'This place is more like a health farm than a hospital,' Alison's husband joked, and Brooke nodded seriously.

'In some ways it is. The emphasis is all on keeping the woman as happy and relaxed as possible.'

Alison bit her lip, her dark eyes worried. 'I'm just afraid that all the breathing and massage in the world won't be enough for me. I know how much of a coward I am when it comes to pain! If I decide to have an epidural, will you think I'm awful?'

'Not at all.' Brooke gave her a reassuring smile. 'We are totally committed to giving the mother the type of birth she wants. If someone is adamant that they want an epidural then we can arrange that. It's nothing to do with bravery, Alison. The pain is different for each person and people cope in different ways, but we never, ever judge anyone, I can assure you of that! Do you have any strong views on the type of delivery you'd like?'

'I did a birth plan.' Alison reached for her bag and pulled out a piece of paper which she handed to Brooke a little hesitantly. 'To be honest, I wasn't sure that you'd want to see it. My midwife said that you don't like them on this unit.'

'Well, she's right in a sense.' Brooke took the birth plan

and tried to explain as carefully as possible. 'The reason is that we've found that some women have set themselves all sorts of goals and expectations and then, when things don't go according to plan, they're disappointed. For example, you might think you don't want any pain relief but when you're in the middle of things you might want to change your mind. We've had a few women who felt that they'd failed and let themselves down by not sticking to their plan, and that was awful. Everyone should be allowed to change their minds at any point.'

Alison nodded and gave a small smile. 'I suppose you don't really know how you'll react to the pain until you experience it.'

'That's right.' Brooke glanced between the couple, her expression serious. 'It's important not to think you have to stick rigidly to what you planned. We do look at birth plans if a woman has made one, but we really like to work with the mother and respond to what she's feeling at the time.'

'That sounds sensible—Ooh.' Alison winced and screwed her fingers round the bedcover as a contraction started to build. 'I never expected the pain to be this bad. Oo-ooh, Tim!'

Her husband stroked her shoulder awkwardly and cast a worried look at Brooke.

'She's fine,' Brooke murmured, moving her palm over the woman's swollen abdomen to feel the strength of the contraction. 'Remember your breathing, Alison. In through your nose and out through your mouth. Perfect. Well done. There—it's tailing off. Now, I just need to examine you. Has anyone explained to you about this machine?'

She moved it slightly closer and ripped off the trace that was hanging down. 'This is called a CTG and it basically tells us about your contractions and your baby's heart rate. At this stage we want you as mobile as possible, so we'll only use it occasionally, just to get a picture of what's happening.'

'Does it look OK? It looks totally incomprehensible to

me.' Alison frowned down at the graph but Brooke nodded and filed it carefully in the notes.

'It's fine. Now, let's take a quick look at this birth plan together.' She read quickly and then glanced up at the couple. 'You seem to be pretty open-minded about most things.'

'I really didn't want to have my membranes ruptured,' Alison murmured, looking at her husband for support, and he nodded firmly.

'That's right. I gather a lot of hospitals do that, but we'd rather let nature take its course.'

'So would we.' Brooke slipped the birth plan into the notes and gave them both a warm smile. 'You're right that some units artificially rupture the membranes the minute the cervix is 4 cm dilated, but we never do that here. We don't rupture membranes, we don't monitor without a reason and we don't do routine internal examinations either. We do them on admission and then when we feel they're necessary.'

Alison's husband frowned. 'But if there's a medical problem?'

'Then we involve our medical team,' Brooke told him promptly. 'That's the good thing about this unit. You get the nearest thing to a home birth without sacrificing the safety of a hospital. Now, then, I'd just like to feel the way the baby is lying, Alison, if that's all right with you.'

She palpated the abdomen carefully, glancing up as Paula slid discreetly into the room and introduced herself to the couple.

'Is it still the right way up?' Alison looked anxious and Brooke nodded with a smile.

'Absolutely. He's coming out head first—what we call a cephalic presentation. And he's nicely flexed so that's good.'

Paula cleared her throat. 'Sister wondered if you'd nip into 4, Brooke. They need some help.'

Brooke glanced at her and caught the urgency of her expression. Trouble, obviously. 'Fine. Well, you're staying with the Neals for the rest of your shift now, aren't you? I'll be back as soon as I can. Just help Alison with her breathing.'

She left the room calmly, and then speeded up as she made for the other delivery room.

'Oh, Brooke—good.' Gill Wilson glanced towards her and then back to her patient. 'Mrs Fox is going to need a section. She's bleeding a bit and we suspect a placental abruption. We've bleeped Mr Matthews, the consultant, and he's meeting us in theatre. Fortunately she's had an epidural so she shouldn't need a general anaesthetic. Is Alison Neal all right for a while if you give me a hand? Suzie needs to go back to her student in 5 so I was hoping you could scrub and take the baby.'

'No problem. Alison's fine with Paula.' Brooke could see from the debris around her that 'bleeding a bit' was something of an understatement, and she knew Gill well enough to know that she was concerned.

Suzie was checking Mrs Fox's blood pressure again. 'Eighty over fifty,' she murmured, and Gill nodded briskly.

'Right. Into theatre.'

Without waiting for a porter, they manipulated the trolley into Theatre where preparations were already under way for an emergency section.

Brooke scrubbed, preparing for her role which was to take the baby once it was delivered, leaving the surgeon to concentrate on the mother. Gill had said the new consultant was good. For the sake of Mrs Fox she hoped that was true. Things weren't looking good.

'How much blood has she lost?' The deep male voice trickled through the doors and Brooke froze.

No. Dear God, no.

She listened again, her heart pounding in her chest. There was a low murmur of voices as Gill replied, and then his voice again. 'OK—we need to get this baby out fast.'

It was him. It was definitely him.

She closed her eyes and struggled to breathe. Six years.

It had been six years since she'd last heard that voice, but she'd have recognised it anywhere. Deep, tough and totally male. Smooth and confident like melted chocolate poured over solid steel. It was the sort of voice that made everyone stop and listen. The sort of voice that was used to issuing orders and commands. And it was the same voice that had once seduced her to within an inch of her life.

Brooke felt her knees shake as panic swamped her. What if he recognised her? No. She had to make sure he didn't. If he ever found out...

Frantically searching for some way of concealing her identity, she noticed a box of masks and grabbed one, hooking it over her ears with shaking fingers. It wasn't a long-term solution but at least it should buy her some time.

She slid into Theatre, her heart thumping, and quickly realised that she needn't have worried. The new consultant wasn't remotely interested in who was standing in his theatre. He was busy, saving two lives.

His hands as steady as a rock, he divided skin and muscle with a speed and skill that made Brooke blink with disbelief. Even in her state of panic she could see that he was good. Incredibly good.

'Is there a paediatrician on the way?' His sharp question was swiftly answered by Gill.

'Dr Patel's on her way down now, Mr Matthews.'

Brooke watched, transfixed, as he stroked through the layers until the uterus was exposed and then made a small transverse incision and passed his right hand into the uterus.

'Out you come, little chap,' he murmured, his eyes flicking up to his SHO who was assisting. 'Press on the fundus.'

Sita Patel arrived just as the newly delivered baby let out an outraged yell, and suddenly Brooke was reaching for the wriggling child, her actions all automatic, her mind still paralysed with shock.

'OK, what have we got here?' The consultant had already turned his attention back to the job in hand. Stopping the bleeding. 'Suction, please. And again... That's better... Oh, yes, I see what's happening...'

Brooke and Sita took charge of the baby, placing it gently on the resuscitaire which had been wheeled into Theatre, so named because it incorporated essential equipment for resuscitating a baby.

'Apgar of 8 at one minute,' Sita murmured, looping the paediatric stethoscope around her neck as Brooke carefully used suction to clear the baby's mouth and nose of mucus. 'He's got good lungs!'

'Is he OK? Is my baby OK?' Mrs Fox was twisting her head anxiously and Jed Matthews gave her a smile, his eyes creasing above the mask.

'He's great—can't you hear that yell? Dr Patel will bring him over just as soon as she's checked him and made him warm. How are things over there, Sita?'

'Fine, Mr Matthews,' Sita replied, finishing her examination of the baby and hovering while Brooke wrapped him up warmly to prevent heat loss. 'He's ready to meet his mum.'

Brooke swallowed. Jed Matthews. She hadn't known his name before today. She allowed herself a brief glance, her heart turning a somersault as she focused on the thick, dark lashes and the brilliant blue eyes visible above the mask. She'd never met a man with eyes like Jed's. Just one look from those very male eyes and she'd drowned...

'Good.' His fingers were still working quickly within the uterine cavity, trying to stop the bleeding. 'How much blood have we got cross-matched, Sister?'

'Two units,' Gill murmured, moving to his side and watching him work.

'Let's give her one unit now, please. Swab.' He reached out a hand and took the sterile swab, frowning down at his handiwork. 'OK, that looks fine. I'm ready to close. Part of your placenta had come away, Mrs Fox, and that was why you were bleeding, but it's fine now. Nothing to worry about.'

Brooke stood immobile, her eyes moving down to those powerful shoulders, clearly outlined by the loose fabric of his theatre greens. How could it be him? How could he be here, of all places?

No longer under pressure, he glanced up and his eyes narrowed as he intercepted her look. For a long moment they stared at each other and Brooke swallowed hard, fighting an overwhelming impulse to turn and run. He hadn't recognised her. He couldn't possibly. Her hair was totally tucked away. Only her eyes were showing. He couldn't have recognised her, could he?

Gill followed his gaze. 'Oh, this is Brooke Daniels, one of our midwives. I didn't have a chance to introduce you earlier—' Suddenly she frowned curiously at Brooke. 'Why on earth are you wearing a mask?'

Trust Gill to notice that little detail. The midwife taking the baby was never near the wound long enough to warrant wearing a mask, but it had been a reflex action because she hadn't wanted Jed to recognise her. She rummaged in her brain for an excuse.

'I've got a bit of a sore throat,' she mumbled, thinking that after the soaking she'd had that morning that comment might well come home to haunt her.

Jed's eyes were still fixed on hers. 'Pleased to meet you, Brooke.'

Was it her imagination or had he really put a slight emphasis on her name?

'I...' She cleared her throat. 'Hello.'

He watched her for another moment, his blue eyes narrowed and quizzical, and then he turned his attention back to the stitching and his patient.

'So, have you chosen a name, Mrs Fox?'

'Ben.' Mrs Fox smiled broadly. 'After my dad.'

Brooke tried to control her trembling knees. Would he recognise her? It had only been one night, after all. One crazy night when she'd allowed herself to be carried away by mistletoe and romance and a man who was straight from every woman's fantasies. A man like him must have been with loads of women since—he was probably even married.

She licked dry lips under her mask and tried to get a grip on her emotions. He wouldn't recognise her. Of course he wouldn't. And if he did, well, she'd just pretend he was mistaken. Yes, that was the best idea. After all, he'd never actually seen her in daylight. Just by candlelight and twinkling Christmas tree lights. And she was hardly that memorable, was she?

Suppressing a groan, she gently lifted the baby back from Mrs Fox and put him in the cot, ready to go to the ward with her. Jed mustn't recognise her, he really mustn't, and if he did...well, she could hardly bring herself to think about the consequences.

'What on earth is the matter with you?' Suzie frowned at her as they checked the controlled-drugs cabinet.

'Nothing.' Brooke opened the book and counted ampoules, her fingers shaking. 'OK, this is the last one. Pethidine.'

'You're like a cat on hot bricks.'

Was she? Only because she was trying to avoid Jed Matthews. Sooner or later he was going to see her without the mask and she'd rather it was later—

Even as she thought it that deep, male drawl came from behind them. 'Anyone free to give me a hand?'

Brooke closed her eyes and kept her back to him. Let Suzie do it. Please?

'I've got to get back to my lady.' Suzie closed the book with a snap. 'But you'll help, won't you, Brooke?'

What choice did she have?

Taking a deep breath, Brooke turned slowly, carefully avoiding looking at him. 'Of course. What did you need, Mr Matthews?'

There was a long silence and when she dared glance at his face their eyes locked and her heart turned over. Dear God, he'd recognised her, she could see it in his eyes.

Something connected between them, something so powerful that she wasn't able to break the contact.

His gaze lifted to her hair and then returned to her eyes, the tension between them so great that Brooke could hardly breathe.

'What did you need me for, Mr Matthews?'

Her words broke the spell and he straightened slightly, his voice rough and very, very male. 'There's a woman in the admissions suite complaining of severe abdominal pain. I need to examine her and I'd like a chaperone, please.'

'Of course.' It was common practice for male doctors to use a chaperone when they examined a patient. 'How pregnant is she?'

With one final glance at her hair Jed Matthews turned on his heel and strode down the corridor. 'Thirty-three weeks. We'll need to examine her and scan her.'

As they walked down the corridor Brooke increased her pace to keep up with his long, easy stride, painfully aware of his closeness. Seeing him again brought back memories that were so vivid they threatened to choke her. He was just how she remembered him. Tall—she guessed him to be about six feet two—with sleek, dark hair swept back from his forehead, and deep blue eyes that were both sexy and sharply observant at the same time. In many ways he was just the same and yet she sensed subtle changes in him. He had an air of authority and calm self-confidence that she didn't remember from their last encounter. Oh he'd been strong even then, but approachable and warm. But now... She closed her eyes briefly and took a deep breath to calm herself. Now she found his cool confidence and overwhelming masculinity almost intimidating.

Brooke followed him into one of the rooms in the admissions suite and stood to one side while he introduced himself to the young mother.

'And when did the pains start, Jane?'

'Midnight.' Jane Duncan bit her lip. 'I haven't been able to lie down or sleep. It's agony, frankly.'

Jed listened carefully and then questioned her further. 'You've had a baby before so you're familiar with the type of pain that goes with labour. Does it feel like labour to you?'

'No.' Jane shook her head. 'Definitely not. Was I wrong to come in?'

'You were absolutely right to come in.' Jed gave her a reassuring smile and walked over to the sink to wash his hands. 'Any pain that keeps you awake all night is worth investigating. I'll examine you internally first and then we'll scan you and fix you up to the monitor for an hour or so to see if it picks anything up. Can I have some gloves, please, Brooke? Size 10.'

Brooke opened the packet and helped settle Jane in the right position.

'Is the baby coming early?' Jane asked, and then winced as Jed examined her.

'Am I hurting you?' He frowned slightly. 'Am I causing the same pain you've been feeling all night?'

'No.' Jane flushed slightly and grabbed Brooke's hand. 'It's a different pain.'

'OK, I've finished.' Jed straightened and gave her an apologetic smile as he ripped off the gloves. 'Sorry to hurt you but I needed to feel your cervix. You're not in labour, Jane. I'm going to scan you now, just to have a look at the baby.'

Brooke wheeled the portable machine to the side of the bed and watched while Jed scanned Jane's abdomen, his gaze fixed on the screen.

'That all looks fine, too, Jane. Baby's heart is fine and he's the right size. Have you felt plenty of movements?'

Jane pulled a face. 'I did until last night. They seemed to tail off but that may have been because I was in too much pain to notice.'

Jed examined her abdomen carefully, palpating the position of the foetus, and then he raised an eyebrow at Brooke.

'Can we put her on the monitor for an hour to see if it shows anything, please?' He turned back to Jane. 'If that looks fine then we'll keep you in for a few hours and then send you home. But come straight back if the pain starts again.'

'I'm not in labour, then?'

He gave her a brief smile. 'Well, not at the moment, but that doesn't mean you're not about to go that way.'

'But it's too early!' Jane's eyes were worried and Jed gave her shoulder a squeeze.

'I'm paid to worry about that, not you. For the time being you're fine.' He walked towards the door and then turned, his eyes on Brooke. 'When you've finished, can I see you in my office, please?'

Brooke nodded, her hands shaking as she attached the various leads to the machine and checked that it was all working.

'There we are.' She managed a smile at Jane. 'That's measuring your baby's heart and any uterine activity. Just relax and read some magazines and I'll be back to check you in about twenty minutes. If you're worried before then, just press the buzzer.'

She left the room and walked towards the consultant's office, her legs shaking. She didn't want to do this, didn't want to see him, but what choice did she have? Judging from the look on his face, if she didn't go voluntarily he'd drag her there himself, and she didn't want to risk a public display.

Tapping on the door, she took a deep breath and tried to control her thumping heart.

He was standing with his back to her, staring out of the window across the wide lawns of the hospital towards the rolling, snow-covered fells beyond.

'Come in, Brooke, and close the door behind you.'

She hesitated and then did as she was told, her hands shaking and her emotions so tangled that she couldn't think clearly. Taking a long, deep breath, she forced herself to calm down. She could handle this. She was an intelligent woman who was more than capable of dealing with the fall-out from one crazy night. For a start, he couldn't prove it was her...

'I've put Mrs Duncan on the monitor and she's—'

'I don't want to talk about Mrs Duncan.' He turned to face her, his eyes flickering to her hand which was within easy reach of the doorknob. An ironic smile touched his handsome features. 'And you can stop hovering by the door, Brooke. This time you're not going anywhere until we've had a talk.'

CHAPTER TWO

Talk?

Jed wanted to talk? She could barely breathe, let alone talk. Just being in the same room as him, almost within touching distance, was more than her will-power could bear. Over the years she'd berated herself repeatedly for her total lack of self-control that night. Never, before or since, had any man made her lose her head the way he had, and in the clear light of day, well away from the burning memories of their shared night, she hadn't been able to understand what had happened to her.

But seeing him now, powerfully male and extravagantly handsome, she could only marvel that she'd managed to walk away from the man at all.

Raising her chin slightly, she gave him a cool smile, relieved that she was wearing trousers. At least he wouldn't be able to see her knees shaking. 'What did you want to talk about, Mr Matthews?'

'Us, Brooke.' His voice was suddenly soft, almost threatening. 'I want to talk about us.'

Her eyes flew to his and she was immediately defensive. She had to protect herself. And not just herself.

'I don't think I understand you, Mr Matthews.'

A hint of a smile touched his firm mouth. 'You understand me perfectly, and before you say anything more you should probably know that in certain circumstances I'm not renowned for my patience.'

That wasn't how she remembered it. He'd shown endless patience on that night, taking things as slowly as she'd needed, showing a touching amount of care for her needs.

'Mr Matthews—'

'My name is Jed.' He spoke slowly, with deliberate emphasis, his eyes never leaving hers for a moment. 'But, then, you can hardly be expected to know that, can you? We didn't exactly spend the night conversing.'

Hot colour seeped into her cheeks. 'I really haven't the slightest idea what you're talking about.'

'You're a lousy liar.' He covered the short distance between them in two easy strides and suddenly he was standing right in front of her, six feet two of powerfully built, very determined male. Startled, Brooke backed away but stopped dead as her shoulders hit the cold, solid wall.

'Nervous?' His eyes lit with grim amusement. 'With good reason. This time there's nowhere to run to. At least, not until I choose to let you. You owe me an explanation.'

'I don't owe you anything.' This time her voice nearly gave her away, and she flinched as his eyes trapped hers.

'Don't play games with me!' His voice was impatient. 'Why did you do it, Brooke? Why did you creep away while I was still asleep? Why did you leave without a word after what we shared that night?'

Suddenly she found she couldn't breathe very well and pushed at his broad chest in an attempt to get herself some space. He didn't budge. She was totally cornered.

'We didn't share anything.' She made one last try, knowing it was futile. This man had a mind like a razor. There was no way she would ever be able to persuade him that he was mistaken. He'd probably never made a mistake in his life. 'It was someone else—'

'You're suggesting I don't know who I've been to bed with?' He raised one dark eyebrow and an ironic smile played around his firm mouth. 'Are you questioning my morals or my memory?'

'Neither.' Her eyes flashed defensively and the panic threatened to choke her. 'I'm just telling you you're mistaken, that's all.'

There was a heavy silence and a muscle worked in his hard jaw.

'Are you seriously trying to convince me that it wasn't you?' He stared at her for a moment and then he started to laugh, a full, masculine sound that made her nerve endings tingle. 'You are hardly easy to forget, Brooke. If you really want to blend into the rest of the female population then you've got some serious work to do.'

Self-consciously she lifted a hand to her dark hair, the wildness of which was still severely curbed by the tight knot she'd constructed that morning. 'I probably just look like someone—'

'Believe me, you don't look like anyone except yourself.' His tone was dry as he reached out and wound a lock of that same dark hair around his fingers.

With a sigh he lifted her stubborn chin with his free hand, forcing her to look at him. 'I've only seen hair like this once in my lifetime. Stop playing games, Brooke.'

She was silent for a moment, her breathing rapid and her mind in a tangle. Suddenly she felt utterly defeated and her slim shoulders sagged. It was too much. On top of everything else it was just too much.

'What are you afraid of?' His voice was suddenly gentle. 'I'm not going to force anything on you that you don't want. I'm not going about to broadcast our relationship around the unit or embarrass you in any way. I just want you to admit the truth.'

And the truth was the one thing she couldn't tell him. She'd decided that six years previously when she'd been forced to face the consequences of their night together...

She made a final attempt, her voice a feeble croak. 'I don't remember you.'

There was a long silence and he gave a soft laugh. 'Shall I tell you something? After that night, my brother Tom was convinced you were Cinderella. Kept trying to persuade me to chase round the hospital on my white charger with a glass slipper tucked under my arm.'

'Well, I'm glad you didn't waste your time.' She pulled herself together with a huge effort and managed a cool smile. 'I can tell you now that it wouldn't have fitted me, Mr Matthews. You've got the wrong woman.'

'We'll see about that, won't we?' His low drawl was intensely masculine and she struggled to control her breathing as he moved closer. Why did he affect her like this? Why?

'You're telling me you found a glass slipper?'

He shook his head slowly, the expression in his eyes making her breath jam in her throat. 'I never looked. I had a much more reliable method of identification up my sleeve.'

His firm mouth hovered tantalisingly close to hers, but before he could move there was a sharp rap on the door and Jed sighed and released her reluctantly, his expression one of mild irritation as he strolled over to the door.

'Yes? Oh, Gill, come in.' He stood to one side as the unit sister walked into his office. 'What can I do for you?'

How could he be so calm and self-contained? Brooke was a nervous wreck and certainly couldn't bring herself to look at her superior. Jed, on the other hand, didn't seem remotely uncomfortable, listening carefully as Gill outlined a problem with one of the patients.

He offered no explanation for Brooke's presence in his office, probably because he knew he wouldn't be questioned, Brooke thought bitterly as she took the chance to slip away, her heart still thumping wildly. Who would question a man like Jed? And it wasn't just because he was the consultant.

Battling for control, she leaned against the wall for a moment, her eyes closed, still seeing the look in his eyes as he'd bent his head towards her.

He'd been about to kiss her. Dear God, if Gill hadn't turned up when she had—

'Are you OK?' Suzie passed her in the corridor and paused. 'You look stunned by something.'

That was an understatement. 'I'm fine.'

'So, what was it like, working with the heartthrob?'

'Heartthrob?' She frowned and Suzie laughed.

'Oh, come on, Brookie! Even you can't be immune to his charms. He's stunning.'

She wasn't immune to his charms, that was the problem. And she never had been.

'If you mean Jed, he's not my type,' she muttered, walking along the corridor to the admissions suite to check on Jane Duncan.

'Not your type?' Suzie stared at her and then smiled slowly. 'Oh, right. Sure. You're one of those women who hate stunningly handsome, rich, successful men—I've read about them, but I've never actually believed they existed until now.'

Brooke gritted her teeth. 'Just leave it, Suzie—'

Suzie opened her mouth and shut it again, her kind eyes suddenly puzzled. 'OK. Sorry.'

'No.' Brooke took a deep breath and gave her friend an apologetic smile. 'I'm the one who should be saying sorry. You're so good to me and I'm a cross-patch. It's just that I'm having a really lousy day.'

Suzie glanced up the corridor and gave her a quick hug. 'What you need is a rich, handsome man who will write a huge cheque and solve all your problems.'

With that she darted off towards one of the delivery rooms, leaving Brooke staring after her.

'No, Suzie,' she murmured softly, tears pricking her dark eyes, 'that is the last thing I need.'

'Well, that looks fine, Jane.' Jed ran his eye carefully over the trace Brooke had handed to him. 'You're not in labour at the moment and there's no point in us keeping you in if the pains have gone.'

'I feel OK now,' Jane admitted. 'What if it happens again?'

'If they're as bad as before then you'd better come straight back.' Jed picked up the notes and tucked them under his arm. 'But let's cross our fingers, shall we?'

Aware that his eyes were on her, Brooke gave him a wary

glance and then wished she hadn't. The message in his intense blue gaze was clear enough. He hadn't finished their conversation. She quickly busied herself helping Jane gather her things together, not relaxing until she heard him leave the room.

'He's gorgeous!' Jane drooled, chattering away as she pulled on her coat. 'Incredibly good-looking. Is he married?'

Brooke forced a smile. If he was then his wife needed to keep a better hold on him. 'I don't know.'

'I expect he is.' Jane laughed and picked up her handbag. 'The good-looking ones are always taken. Lucky wife, having a man like that to take care of her.'

Brooke felt her heart twist and held open the door. Thank goodness they were so busy, Brooke thought as she saw Jed striding off towards Theatre again, followed by his SHO and a flock of medical students. At least it postponed the inevitable confrontation. She didn't kid herself for one minute that Jed was going to let the matter drop. That one look had said it all.

'Brooke?' Paula, the student midwife she'd left with Alison Neal, was hovering in the corridor anxiously. 'I could do with a hand if you've got a minute. Alison's getting very distressed and I can't seem to calm her down at all.'

Brooke gave a nod and a brief smile. At least work was a constant distraction. 'I'll come now. What pain relief has she had so far?'

'Just gas and air.' Paula looked stressed and worried. 'But she's really panicky and I can't seem to relax her at all.'

Brooke followed her into the birthing room and walked straight over to Alison who was sitting on the edge of the bed, breathing rapidly, her hair hanging in damp tendrils over her forehead.

'How are you doing?' Brooke sat down next to her and slipped an arm round the woman's shoulders, feeling the tension under her fingers.

'I never imagined it would be this painful.' Alison's

breaths were coming in pants and her cheeks were pale and stained with tears. 'Breathing just doesn't seem to work and the gas and air makes me feel sick. I'm no good at this.'

'You're doing brilliantly,' Brooke said quietly, taking charge of the situation and glancing at Paula. 'Can you draw the curtains, please? Let's darken the room and try and make the atmosphere more relaxing. Alison, I'm going to use some aromatherapy oils to try and help you relax.'

Alison's husband frowned. 'Are they safe in labour?'

'The ones we use are.' Brooke stood up and reached into a cupboard for the vaporiser which was kept in each delivery room. 'Generally we stick to lavender and clary but sometimes I use nutmeg.'

'How on earth do you know all that?' Alison looked at her, momentarily distracted. 'Are you a trained aromatherapist?'

'Yes, actually,' Brooke admitted with a smile. 'Lots of midwives are these days. There's a general move towards a more holistic approach to pregnancy and birth, and quite a few have done the necessary training to offer aromatherapy to women in labour. We're very lucky that the unit here encourages that sort of thing.'

Brooke added the oils to the vaporiser and the room was soon filled with the soothing smell of essential oils.

'Oh, that's nice.' Alison closed her eyes and breathed deeply, dropping her head onto her chest as another pain ripped through her body. 'Here we go again...'

Brooke sat beside her and massaged her gently, talking her quietly through the pain and helping her to breathe properly. When the pain was over Brooke turned to Alison's husband.

'It might help if you massaged her back for her.'

He looked helpless. 'What do I do?'

Together they helped Alison straddle a chair and Brooke showed him how to do thumb-circling on the shoulders using an oil mixture blended with essential oils.

'Oh, that feels so good, Tim...' Alison gave a moan of

pleasure and closed her eyes, breathing deeply as her husband gently massaged her skin. 'Tell me you'll do this when I'm not in labour.'

Tim Neal gave a self-conscious grin. 'As long as you don't expect me to go and train as an aromatherapist.'

Brooke stayed with them and monitored Alison's contractions, and although she was more relaxed it was obvious that she was still finding the pain hard to bear.

'Would you consider using the pool?' Brooke crouched down in front of her, her eyes kind and gentle. 'Many women find it a great pain-reliever, you know.'

Alison shook her head, tears welling up in her eyes. 'I don't fancy it. I'm sorry, I know it's illogical...'

'It doesn't matter,' Brooke said quietly. 'I'm just trying to find something that suits you because I think you do need something more, don't you?'

Alison nodded and the tears slipped onto her cheeks. 'I'm such a wimp.'

'You're not a wimp, Alison, far from it. You're doing marvellously.' Brooke sat cross-legged on a cushion and glanced from one to the other. 'Would you like to consider an epidural?'

'Paula was just telling us that there is a greater risk of forceps delivery if I have an epidural.' Alison shifted on the chair, looking uncomfortable and anxious. 'I really don't know what to do.'

'Well, it's true that there's a higher incidence of what we call an assisted delivery—that's forceps or ventouse—with an epidural in place. That's because you're not always able to feel the urge to push so well when your lower half is numb. But there's always the option of allowing the epidural to wear off when you're ready to push.'

Alison frowned and raked her tangled hair away from her face. 'And does that work?'

'Not always,' Brooke admitted, resting her chin on her palm as she looked at Alison. 'We can make a good guess as to how quickly you'll dilate, but some labours can be unpredictable so there's no guarantee that we can time it perfectly. And some women find it hard to have been pain-free and then suddenly have strong contractions with no build-up.'

'The truth is, I really want an epidural, but I know midwives hate them.' Alison bit her lip. 'You'd rather I tried to do it by myself, wouldn't you?'

'Not at all. If you'd like an epidural then that's fine by me. I would need to examine you because we can't give you an epidural until you're at least three centimetres dilated or it can stop your labour, and we don't want to have to interfere with drips and things.'

Alison glanced at her husband and swallowed hard. 'I think I would like one.'

'That's fine, then.' Brooke rose to her feet. 'Let's get you back on the bed so that I can examine you, and we'll take it from there.'

Ten minutes later she'd ascertained that Alison was five centimetres dilated and well able to have an epidural.

'You're doing really well but you have still got a way to go. The head's in a good position so I don't foresee any problems at the moment. Would you like to go for it?'

Alison looked helplessly at her husband and then back at Brooke. 'I said I wasn't having anything, but that was before I knew what it felt like.'

'It doesn't matter to me, love,' Tim assured her, giving his wife a quick kiss. 'You do what feels right.'

Brooke sat down on the bed next to her, her expression sympathetic. 'You know, there really isn't a right and a wrong way, Alison. You have to do what feels right to you.'

Tears slipped down Alison's cheeks. 'I don't know. It feels like agony and I'm starting to panic about the delivery itself.'

'Nothing to panic about,' Brooke soothed. 'Just think about now. Let's work through a few more contractions together and see how you cope.'

She spent another twenty minutes with Alison, at the end

of which everyone decided that an epidural was the right option because she was so adamant that she wouldn't use the pool.

Paula caught up with Brooke in the corridor as she went to bleep the anaesthetist.

'You're brilliant with her. I couldn't get her to relax at all.'

Brooke gave her a tired smile. 'Don't blame yourself. She's very, very anxious.'

'Is that why you encouraged her to go for the epidural?'

'She wanted one,' Brooke said simply, picking up the phone and dialling Switchboard. 'She just needed reassurance that we wouldn't disapprove of her choice.'

'But generally you do try to encourage them to avoid medical intervention?'

'What we really encourage is freedom of choice for the mother,' Brooke told her, tucking the receiver under her ear. 'We want them to have as much choice as possible in their labour and delivery. Alison is clearly not happy about using the pool and she's in a lot of pain. An epidural is probably right for her. Switch? Can you bleep Dr Penny for me, please?'

'I'll need to do regular obs, won't I?' Paula scribbled in her notebook and Brooke nodded as she replaced the receiver.

'Yes. An epidural can lower the blood pressure dramatically. I'll leave you for now but give me a yell when Dr Penny arrives and I'll give you a hand.'

The afternoon flew by and Brooke was rushed off her feet, helping students, admitting pregnant women in labour and arranging transfers to the ward.

'You OK, Brooke?' Gill caught up with her halfway through the afternoon.

Brooke rubbed her aching neck. 'Yes, I suppose. I miss spending an entire shift with one woman.' She exchanged a rueful glance with the senior sister.

'Yes, well, that's today's NHS for you.' Gill sighed and

checked her watch. 'I hate to ask you this, Brooke, and I suppose your circumstances will make it impossible, but—'

'Will I work a double shift?' Brooke chanted, rolling her eyes. 'Yes, of course I will.'

Gill's eyes narrowed. 'You're sure? I thought you might have to rush back.'

'No. Not tonight.'

'Well, that's great. Thanks a lot. How's Mrs Neal coming along?'

Brooke pulled a face. 'Slowly. I've just bleeped the anaesthetist.'

'Right. Let me know when she's delivering.'

Alison Neal continued to make slow progress and by six o'clock she was fully dilated and had been pushing for an hour. As it was her first baby, in theory she could have been left to push for longer but Brooke was worried about the baby.

'His heart rate is dipping slightly with each contraction, Alison, so I'm going to give the doctor a ring.'

Bother. She was going to have to ring Jed because his SHO didn't have enough experience, the registrar was off sick and the senior reg wasn't due to start for another six weeks.

He strode into the room five minutes later and Brooke immediately handed him the trace, dispensing with preliminaries.

'We're getting late decelerations.' She knew that if the baby's heart rate dropped after the peak of a contraction it could be a sign that the baby was short of oxygen. 'I've tried changing her position but it's made no difference.'

'Right.' Jed frowned down at the trace, and slipped the paper through his fingers, examining it in detail. 'How many centimetres dilated is she now?'

'She's fully dilated and she's been pushing for an hour, but the head's still quite high.'

'OK.' Jed handed the trace back to her and smiled at the

Neals. 'I'm Jed Matthews, the consultant. How are you doing?'

'I've been better.' Alison was looking exhausted, her blonde hair hanging limply round her shoulders. 'What happens now?'

'I'd like to examine you,' Jed said gently, 'and then we'll decide together what's best.'

Alison nodded and Brooke gestured to Paula to help Jed as she settled herself on the bed and talked quietly to Alison.

Jed snapped on a pair of gloves and examined Alison carefully, his face a mask of concentration.

'OK.' His handsome face was thoughtful as he finished his examination and gave Alison a warm smile. 'It's hard to know who's more tired, you or the baby.'

Alison's grip tightened on Brooke's hand and she and her husband exchanged anxious glances. 'Is he in trouble?'

Jed hesitated, choosing his words carefully. 'Not yet, but we need to deliver him as quickly as we can. Have you heard of a ventouse delivery?'

Alison took a deep breath. 'That's the suction thing, isn't it?'

Jed nodded. 'Basically, yes. I attach a flexible cap to the baby's head and when you push, I give you a bit of extra help. You're still doing most of the work, but I can give you a helping hand.'

Brooke blinked with admiration. Somehow he'd managed to make it seem as though Alison would still be doing it all herself. Clever man.

'Will it hurt?' Alison looked suddenly anxious and Jed shook his head, his eyes kind as he moved over to the sink and started to scrub.

'Your epidural was topped up not long ago so, to be honest, it shouldn't, and I'll be as gentle as I possibly can.'

Seeing Alison's expression, Brooke decided that Jed's bedside manner was second to none but, then, she already knew that, didn't she? Remembering just exactly how skilled Jed's bedside manner was brought a blush to her cheeks and she dragged her mind back to work with an effort.

'Paula, would you bleep the paediatrician and then assist Mr Matthews, please? I'll sit with Alison.'

Alison grabbed her hand tightly. 'Will you stay with me the whole time?'

'The whole time,' Brooke promised, hoping that Jed was as skilled at using the ventouse as he was at performing emergency Caesarean sections.

He was. As soon as she and Tim had manoeuvred Alison into the right position, Jed applied the cup to the baby's head with enviable ease. He glanced over his shoulder at Paula.

'Have you seen this before?'

She shook her head and he raised an eyebrow. 'Well, stand a bit closer, then, and I'll tell you what I'm doing.'

Paula blushed and did as she was told, sneaking a glance at the broad shoulders as she moved to where he'd indicated she should stand.

Noticing the look, Brooke felt a stab of jealousy which she quickly suppressed. What was the matter with her? Why should she be jealous?

Brooke watched as Jed applied traction, explaining quietly to Paula and talking occasionally to Alison who had Brooke's hand in a vice-like grip.

'It's important not to use excessive traction,' he murmured, using the force of the contraction to help his own efforts. 'It's descending nicely. Well done, Alison. We'll soon have this baby out. What's the heart rate doing, Brooke?'

Brooke glanced at the CTG machine and met his eyes. Frankly, it wasn't good but she didn't want to panic Alison.

'Eighty,' she said flatly, and Jed nodded, comprehension in his blue eyes.

'Right. One big push for me, Alison. Come on, baby.' He pulled gently and the head emerged, blue and mottled, just as Sita slid discreetly into the room with the necessary equipment.

'OK, I've finished with the ventouse now. Well done, Alison.' Jed worked quickly, removing the cup and getting ready to deliver the rest of the baby. 'Here he comes.'

The baby slithered into his waiting hands and he lifted it smoothly onto Alison's abdomen, grinning as it started to yell.

'I love that sound!'

Brooke breathed a sigh of relief and grinned at him, momentarily forgetting the tension between them. She loved that sound, too.

'Oh, Alison!' Tim Neal's voice was choked with emotion as he gently touched his new baby, and Brooke blinked several times. Bother! Why was she always such a marshmallow?

Fifteen minutes later the cord was cut, the placenta delivered and mother and baby were cuddled up together as if they'd known each other for ever.

'Well, you didn't need me here at all,' Sita declared cheerfully, having checked the baby and pronounced it well.

'Thank you.' Tears misted Alison's eyes as she looked at Jed. 'You were brilliant, wasn't he, Tim?'

Her husband looked shell-shocked by the whole experience. 'He certainly was.'

'Don't tell him that. It's crowded enough in the labour ward without having a doctor with an oversized head,' Brooke quipped, helping Paula clear up after the delivery. But he had done well, she had to admit it. He'd managed to deliver the baby with the minimum of fuss but she'd seen the skill in his technique.

'She's gorgeous.' Jed smiled down at the baby and touched its tiny cheek with one strong finger.

Brooke froze, her eyes fixed on his face.

'Do you have children, Doctor?' Alison smiled up at him and Jed shook his head.

'Not yet. But one day I hope to.'

Suddenly Brooke felt as though she was suffocating and she mumbled an excuse and left the room.

Dear God, what was she going to do? How was she going to handle this?

It was nearly ten o'clock by the time the labour ward had calmed down, and as she changed and dragged on her coat Brooke felt exhausted. The prospect of a bus ride home filled her with gloom. What on earth was she going to do about the stupid car?

Pushing the worry aside, she stuck her head round the office door and smiled at Gill. 'I'm off. My bus goes in five minutes.'

'Thanks, Brooke!'

Brooke gathered up her bits and pieces from the staffroom and dashed out of the hospital, sprinting across the car park as she saw the lights of the bus approach.

'Brooke!'

No! She stopped dead and turned, eyeing the low, expensive sports car and Jed Matthews with frustration. What was it like to have a car that started?

'Not now, Mr Matthews. I'm already late.' She turned and ran for the bus, her heart bursting as she crossed the lawn just in time to see it pull away. 'No! No, no, no!'

Tears pricked her eyes and she slammed her bag down onto the seat and sat down next to it. Suddenly it was all too much and the tears slid down her cheeks. Damn. She never cried! Never! Brushing them away with the back of her hand, she gave herself a sharp telling-off. How pathetic! She was just tired, that was all. Tired. Nothing more.

Strong fingers curled into her shoulder and pulled her upright.

'Get in.' Jed propelled her towards his car. 'I'll give you a lift home.'

'No! I don't want a lift!' She shook herself free and glared at him, her eyes still shiny with tears. 'Just leave me alone, will you? I don't need you here on top of everything else!! First the heating, then the roof and now the car, and I missed my bus...'

She choked on the lump in her throat and, before she could protest, strong arms had swept her off her feet and deposited her in the passenger seat. Warmth and comfort enveloped her and she sagged against the plush seat, the fight draining out of her like water through a sieve.

'I don't want a lift,' she mumbled, her dark lashes clogged with tears as Jed leaned across her to fasten her seat belt. The urge to touch him was so strong it was a physical pain. She could see the dark shadow of his jaw and smell that tantalising male scent that she remembered so well. Dear God, she loved this man. She'd loved him from the first minute she'd stared into those sexy blue eyes, and she'd never stopped loving him even though she knew it was hopeless.

'Where to?' He pulled out of the hospital car park and drove slowly towards the main road, glancing at her expectantly.

She rallied her flagging spirits and fumbled for the door-handle. 'I don't want you to take me home. I don't want to go anywhere with you.'

'Unless you want to add to your problems by falling out of a moving car, I suggest you leave the door shut,' he drawled, picking up speed so that she had no choice but to release the handle.

'You're a bully.'

'Stop behaving like a child and give me some directions.' His words were clipped, his expression exasperated. 'Brooke, you missed your bus and I'm taking you home. It's as simple as that. Now, do I turn left or right?'

'I don't want to go home with you.' For some reason the tears wouldn't stop flowing and she hated herself for it.

'Left or right?' This time his voice was gentler and he paused at the junction with the main road and dug a hand in his pocket, handing her a tissue.

She took it and blew her nose hard. Oh, what was the

point in fighting with him? She needed to get home and this was as good a way as any. 'Right. Take the road towards Elterwater.'

'Progress!' He slammed his foot on the accelerator and the car sped along the quiet roads, making a soft purring sound that Brooke had never heard before. Her car made the oddest noises. Bangs and grinding noises. Nothing like this. Maybe this was what a car was meant to sound like when it worked.

His eyes were fixed on the road ahead. 'So, how long have you lived up here?'

'In the Lake District?' She pushed the tissue up her sleeve. 'Two years.'

'Why did you move from London?'

'I needed—' She broke off and glared at his profile. 'Who said I was in London?'

He gave a sigh, his dark hair glossy in the moonlight. 'Are you always this defensive? Relax, Brooke. You won't be giving anything away. I know who you are and I know you worked in London. Why did you move?'

For a hundred reasons, none of which she could tell him. 'I like the country.'

'Right.' He glanced at her, one eyebrow lifted. 'Where now?'

'Left at this junction and then right up the hill. My cottage is first on the right. Or at least it was when I left it this morning,' she said dryly. 'Knowing my luck, it's probably fallen down by now.'

He laughed but he gave her a keen look as he pulled the car to a halt. 'That bad, huh?'

'You have no idea,' Brooke muttered under her breath, releasing her seat belt and giving him the best smile that she could manage. 'Thanks for the lift.'

She scrambled out of the car, thinking that sports cars weren't that easy to get out of, and slammed the door, her eyes narrowing as he did the same thing.

'What do you think you're doing?'

His eyes glinted at her across the roof of the car. 'Coming in to finish the conversation.'

'No way!' She didn't want him in her house. There were too many clues in there. She swung her bag over her shoulder and glared at him as she marched past him and made for her front door. 'It's late and I want to go to bed.'

Bother! Why on earth had she said that? The look in his eyes brought the colour to her cheeks but thankfully he didn't make the obvious remark.

'We need to talk, Brooke.' His voice was low and very, very male. 'Preferably without an audience.'

Her hand shook as she tried to get the key in the lock. 'We have nothing to talk about.'

The key turned at last and she pushed open the door and turned to say a firm goodbye, but he was already shouldering his way past her into the narrow hall of her cottage.

'How dare you?' She stared at him, outraged. 'You can't just barge in here and take over my life.'

'I'm not taking over your life.' Jed's voice was calm and slightly amused. 'Calm down. I don't want anything from you except a conversation.'

'Yes, well, after the day I've had I'm not up to conversation.' Suddenly exhausted, Brooke dropped her bag in the hall and closed the front door. How was she going to keep her secret, with him prowling round her house?

Marching past him without a glance, she took the stairs two at a time and braced herself for the worst. What had a whole day of rain done to her house?

Gingerly she pushed open the door and gasped in horror as she saw the overflowing bucket. Replacing it quickly with an empty one, she sank back on her heels and stared helplessly at the ceiling.

'So this is the roof bit of your problem?' Jed lounged in her doorway, surveying the damage through narrowed eyes.

'Sorry?' Brooke glanced nervously at him but reassured herself that there was nothing in this room to give him any clues as to who normally slept there. She'd emptied it out as soon as the roof had started to leak.

'When I picked you up you said, "First the heating, then the roof and now the car." Presumably this is the roof bit of the problem.'

Brooke nodded and braced herself to lift the brimming bucket.

'I'll do that.' He took it from her easily and deposited it in the bathroom. 'How long has it been like this?'

'Since the weekend.'

He frowned. 'Wouldn't anyone come and see to it?'

Probably, if she could have afforded to pay them, Brooke thought grimly.

'They're coming on Saturday.' After payday.

He squinted up at her ceiling. 'It's probably nothing much. Just a few tiles missing. What happened with the heating?'

'It broke.' Nothing behind her words betrayed the cost of having it fixed.

'And the car?'

She managed a smile. 'Well, let's just say that broke, too. I'm having a really good week.'

His eyes searched hers for a moment and then flickered back to the bedroom ceiling. 'Is it your house?'

'Yes, for my sins. If it was rented at least I could threaten the landlord.'

There was a slight pause. 'You don't have a man in your life?'

She swallowed and shook her head. What was the point in lying? 'No. And, anyway, I don't see what difference that would make. Now, will you go and leave me alone?'

He didn't budge. 'I could probably help with that roof—'

She lifted her chin. 'I don't need help, but thanks for the offer.'

He stood aside to let her pass. 'From where I'm standing, Brooke, it looks as though you need all the help you can get.'

She reached the bottom of the stairs and turned to face him, her eyes blazing. 'If you've finished what you came to say, you can go now.'

He shook his head and closed the distance between them, his powerful frame dominating her narrow hallway.

'I haven't even started.'

Brooke swallowed. 'We have nothing to say to each other, Jed—'

'I've got plenty to say. I want to know why you left me that night.' He was standing so close to her that she could hardly breathe. She felt smothered, totally surrounded by his male presence.

'I don't know what you mean—I've already told you it wasn't me.'

He swore softly and a muscle worked in his lean jaw. 'So we're back to the glass-slipper routine, are we? All right, then let's see if it fits.'

His strong hands slid into her hair and held her face firmly while his mouth came down on hers.

CHAPTER THREE

Jed's kiss.

The demands of his mouth sent a wicked thrill surging through Brooke's body, and she forgot everything except how this man could make her feel.

It had been six years.

Six years since that incredible night, but nothing had changed between them. His kiss still had the power to control her. To cloud her head with wild excitement. To make her want what she couldn't have.

With devastating precision his mouth seduced hers, rough and yet not hurting her, an all-consuming act of male possession stirring her senses until her head swam.

Jed's kiss.

Jed's kiss was the reason she'd acted out of character that night. His kiss had made her discover a part of herself that she hadn't known was there, and his kiss was the reason she'd run from him.

Drugged by the touch of his mouth, she murmured a protest as he lifted his dark head and would have lost her balance if he hadn't steadied her.

He still held her face, forcing her to meet his gaze.

'Well, Cinderella...' His voice was deep and husky. 'I'd say the slipper fits perfectly. Wouldn't you?'

She closed her eyes, hating her weakness and her reaction to him. Why did it have to be this way? Never before and never since had any man made her feel the way he did.

She swallowed hard and opened her eyes. 'Jed—'

'Scary, isn't it?' He was looking at her with total comprehension. 'What happens between us is so powerful it's scary.'

'You're just a good kisser.' Her voice shook as she tried to casually dismiss what had happened between them.

'You think so?' He smiled and his eyes teased her gently. 'You think that happens with every woman I kiss?'

She blushed. 'Well, yes—why shouldn't it?'

'Are you really still that innocent?' His voice was soft and he gave a sigh and pulled her against him, running his hands up her back. 'It isn't anything I do, Brooke. It's us. Something we create together. What happens between you and me is like a miracle, and I can assure you I've never felt it with a single other woman.'

She stared at him, her heart thumping. She had to ask— had to know. 'Are you married?'

'Married?' He looked stunned by the question and then lifted a brow, a smile playing around his firm mouth. 'You think I could kiss a woman like that if I was married to someone else? Ouch.'

'I don't know what to think, Jed.' She shook her head slowly and pushed at his hard chest. 'Let me go. Please?'

He released her immediately but didn't move away, his powerful body still tantalisingly close to hers.

Brooke forced herself to accept the inevitable. This man wasn't going anywhere until they'd had a conversation. Her lips still tingling from his kiss, she turned and walked towards the kitchen.

'Do you want a drink? I've got lager or white wine.' Her tone was sharper than she'd intended but he didn't react.

'Lager is great.' He shifted one of her kitchen chairs and straddled it, his keen blue eyes watching her every move. 'So, are you still pretending you don't know me?'

What was the point? She gave a sigh and shook her head, before delving into her fridge and pulling out a can of lager and handing it to him.

'Do you want a glass?'

'No, thanks.' His eyes searched hers as he opened the can. 'Was it a shock, seeing me again?'

'Are you kidding?' She made a valiant attempt at humour.

'After the heating, the roof and the car? Nothing shocks me any more.'

'But you didn't want to see me again, did you?' His voice was suddenly soft. 'Or you wouldn't have left while I was still asleep.'

She coloured furiously and turned away, picking up the kettle and filling it. 'I don't want to talk about it, Jed. I've admitted it was me. Now let's leave it at that.'

'No way. Tell me you don't think about it.' His voice was husky and teased her senses. 'Tell me you never think about that night.'

'Jed, stop it!' The kettle clattered onto the side and she covered her ears, trying not to listen to him, but he refused to let her hide from him.

'Tell me you don't lie awake at night, remembering what it was like between us.'

Suddenly he was standing right behind her, his warm breath teasing the back of her neck as he pulled her hands away from her ears. 'We couldn't stop, Brooke, do you remember that? It was like a fever, a desperation—'

'No!' She interrupted him frantically, shaking her head and denying everything he was saying. 'No! Just drop it, Jed!'

'Not on your life. I've waited for six years to find out why you ran off that night.'

There was a long silence while she tried to control her breathing. 'I didn't run. I just left. It was morning.'

'And I was still asleep,' he pointed out gently, his strong fingers holding her shoulders.

'Why shouldn't I leave?' Her small chin lifted defensively. 'It was just a fling, Jed—a one-night stand. People don't hang around to talk about sweet nothings.'

'Don't they?' A muscle worked in his cheek and his eyes narrowed. 'And how would you know, Brooke? How many one-night stands have you had in your life?'

She closed her eyes and shook her head, her dark hair

escaping from the pins that held it in place. 'Just leave me alone. Please.'

'No way.' He shook his head and stood directly in front of her, so close that she could feel the warmth of his body brushing hers. 'I'm not leaving you alone now. Look at me!'

She ignored his gentle command and stiffened as she felt him slide strong hands up her arms.

'Dammit, Brooke, will you look at me?' He cupped her face and forced her to look at him. 'I can't believe I've found you again after so long, and if you think I'm going to waste time playing games then you've got another think coming.'

Every sense in her body was in turmoil as she struggled with her feelings. 'Jed, I don't want this—'

'I don't believe you,' he said succinctly. 'I realise that something is holding you back and I'm waiting very patiently for you to tell me what. You've told me you're not married. Are you involved with someone? Is that it?'

Her breathing was uneven and she lifted her chin, her eyes suddenly angry. 'You're so arrogant, do you know that?!' Her eyes blazed into his, her breathing so rapid she was virtually panting. 'Just because I'm probably the first woman who's ever left your bed before you were ready, you assume that there must have been a complicated reason. Maybe I just didn't like you enough. Have you thought of that?'

'No, I haven't.' Far from seeming offended by her words, he looked almost amused.

'Well, maybe you should start thinking of that,' she said flatly, her chin lifting as a smile touched his firm mouth.

'If you don't mind me saying so, it was pretty strange behaviour for someone who didn't like me.' His tone was deceptively mild and he caught her chin in his strong fingers. 'But maybe you've forgotten exactly what happened that night. Shall I jog your memory?'

Dear God, no! That was the last thing she needed. 'Jed, please—'

'We connected instantly, do you remember that? Eyes across a crowded dance floor, just like the best romantic movies. Then we danced, first at the ball, then outside under the Christmas-tree lights and the stars. And then, when we couldn't bear the torment any longer, we went back to my flat.'

'That's enough!' She thumped at his broad chest but he caught her wrists and held her easily.

'We didn't make it to the bed, did we, Brooke?' His voice was soft and insistent. 'We just about managed to close the front door, but that was it.'

'You're making it into something it wasn't!' Brooke was frantic. 'It was just a one-night stand, Jed. People have them all the time.'

'Do they?' His tone was flat and his eyes locked with hers. 'I don't. That was the first and only time in my life I've gone to bed with a woman I didn't know, but shall I tell you something? I did know you. From the minute I saw you I felt as though I'd known you all my life. And what about you? How many one-night stands had you had before that night?'

Brooke felt tears prick her eyes and she shook her head, unable to answer.

'Shall I tell you?' His voice was low and very male and his fingers tightened on her arms. 'None. You'd never even been to bed with a man before, so don't try telling me that it didn't mean anything to you.'

Hot colour seeped into her cheeks and she looked away from him. 'You don't know that.'

'Brooke...' He gave a sigh and lifted her chin, his blue eyes unbelievably gentle. 'Believe me, I do know that. You were a virgin, sweetheart.'

She closed her eyes, embarrassed by the intimacy of his words. 'I'd like you to go now.'

There was a short silence. 'Why?'

She opened her eyes and looked straight into his. 'You

wanted this conversation, not me. Well, now it's over and I'd like you to leave.'

He shook his head, his mouth a grim line. 'Not without an explanation.'

'OK, I'll give you an explanation!!' Her heart was pounding so fast she felt dizzy. 'I panicked, Jed! I left because I panicked. Before that night I had never been to bed with a man—to be honest, I'd never even really had a proper boyfriend. What happened with you scared me. I couldn't believe what I'd done—I needed time to think.'

She broke off, breathless, and Jed frowned.

'I can understand that, I suppose. But once you'd had time to think, you must have seen that what we had was special. So why didn't you track me down?'

Brooke avoided his gaze. Because of the discovery she'd made a few weeks later. A discovery that had totally wiped out her fantasy about having a relationship with him. It had made everything impossible.

'Surely you'd—' He broke off, frowning suddenly over her shoulder. 'What's that?'

'What's what?' Thrown by the change of subject, she glanced behind her and froze. Oh, dear God. She'd thought all the clues had been tidied away. But she'd forgotten about her walls.

'"To Mummy with love from Toby"?' He read it slowly, his eyes taking in every aspect of the childish painting, and then he looked back at her. '"Mummy"? Are you "Mummy"?'

Her voice didn't seem to work properly, and when it did it croaked. 'Yes.'

'You have a child?'

She nodded, suddenly mute.

There was a long silence while he stared at the picture, his expression unreadable.

'Boy or girl?'

What did it matter? 'Boy.' She cleared her throat. 'His name is Toby.'

A muscle worked in his lean jaw. 'How old?'

'He's five.' Actually, he was nearly six but she was hoping she'd get away with being unspecific. At least until she'd had time to work out what she was going to do. Brooke knew what Jed was thinking and her heart started to race. Was he going to ask her a direct question?

'Five.' His eyes locked with hers and she could see him doing the sums. 'So tell me, Brooke, was he born nine months after you spent the night with me?'

'No.' She managed to hold his gaze steadily. After all, she was telling the truth. 'No, Jed, he wasn't.'

For a moment he looked stunned and then his eyes hardened. 'Which means he was born nine months after you spent the night with someone else...'

She flinched at his tone. 'That's none of your business.'

He stood still for a long time, his dark jaw rigid as he stared at the picture and then he glanced down at her, his blue eyes cold. 'You may not have had any experience before you met me, but you certainly didn't waste any time afterwards, did you? You're right.' The words were clipped. 'It isn't any of my business. You're obviously not the woman I thought you were. Goodnight, Brooke.'

He turned on his heel and strode out of the cottage without a backward glance.

'You look pale—are you all right?' Gill frowned at Brooke who managed a smile.

'I'm fine,' she lied, wishing she'd spent longer on her make-up. She didn't want everyone commenting on the fact that she'd had no sleep. 'Where do you want me?'

'Jed Matthews is in 2. Could you help him—?'

'No!' The words flew out before she could stop them and Brooke bit her lip. 'I'm sorry. I didn't mean—I just fancied doing a plain, ordinary delivery with no medical intervention.'

And no contact with Jed Matthews.

Gill gave her a keen look. 'Well, they don't seem to be

very much in evidence at the moment, but you can swap with Suzie and take the woman in 5 if you like. Suzie, will you help Mr Matthews?'

'Of course.' Suzie gave a willing smile and tucked her pen in her pocket. 'I'll do my best not to drool all over him.'

'Do that,' Gill advised dryly, picking up the phone as soon as it rang. 'Labour Ward, Sister speaking.' She frowned slightly as she listened. 'Oh, dear, I'm sorry to hear that, Mrs Duncan. Yes, you'd better come straight in.'

She replaced the receiver and pulled a face at Brooke. 'Sorry. That was Jane Duncan who you looked after yesterday. She's started to bleed so she's coming straight back in. You'll have to look after her, I'm afraid, and I'll put the student in 5.'

Brooke licked dry lips. 'That's fine, Gill, no problem.'

'Good.' The sister gave her a keen look. 'I'll warn Mr Matthews.'

Jane Duncan arrived ten minutes later, her face pale and anxious. 'I've been bleeding—'

'Just settle yourself on the bed and we'll take a look at you,' Brooke said gently, taking her bag from her and smiling at her husband. 'Have a seat while I settle your wife, Mr Duncan.'

Jane flopped onto the bed, looking terrified. 'Does the bleeding mean I'm in labour?'

'Not necessarily.' Brooke handed her a gown and drew the curtains round the bed. 'Mr Matthews examined you internally yesterday and that can sometimes cause a bleed. How much was it?'

'Quite a bit.' Jane shifted as she pulled on the gown. 'I kept the pad.'

'Well done. Very sensible.' Brooke helped her fold her clothes and checked her blood pressure and temperature. 'That's all fine, Jane. Try not to panic. I'll go and tell Mr Matthews you're here.'

'Sister's already told me.' The deep male voice made her

shoulders stiffen. 'Hello, Jane.' Jed's eyes were kind as they flickered to the anxious woman. 'Let's take another look at you and see what's going on, shall we? Brooke, I'll need to examine her again, and can you do a trace, please?'

Brooke nodded and fetched him what he needed, at the same time giving herself a sharp talking-to. What did it matter if he was cold with her? If he believed that she'd— that she'd—

'Brooke!' His sharp tone cut through her thoughts and she realised that he'd been speaking to her.

'I'm sorry...'

'I said that the cervix feels different to yesterday so we'd better be on the safe side and give her some betamethasone.' He scribbled on the chart and handed it to Brooke. 'Give her 25 mg now and another 25 mg in 12 hours. I'm going to give you some steroids, Jane.'

Jane looked anxious. 'Steroids? Why steroids?'

Jed propped one foot on the bottom rung of the bed as he talked to the couple. 'There's very good evidence that given before 34 weeks' gestation they help your baby's lungs mature. There's a chance this baby may come early so we want to give him all the help we can. Basically the steroids help the baby's breathing.'

Jane's husband frowned. 'I've heard of respiratory distress syndrome...'

'Right.' Jed gave a nod. 'Well, steroids have been shown to reduce the incidence of RDS. At the moment we're not sure that Jane is going to go into labour but we're not taking any chances.'

'And if she doesn't go into labour?' Mr Duncan was understandably protective of his wife, and Jed took plenty of time to explain the position in detail. Even Brooke had to admit that as an obstetrician he was amazingly skilful and sensitive with the mums. It was just with her that he didn't give an inch.

'The steroids won't do any harm,' Jed assured them, his eyes flicking over her notes quickly. 'You're thirty-three weeks now, Jane. We'll admit you to the ward and see what happens. Stay in bed and relax.'

Jane gave a sigh and nodded. 'I haven't got much choice, have I?'

'I'm afraid not.' Jed smiled sympathetically and handed the notes to Brooke. 'Would you arrange for her to be admitted, please?'

It took half an hour for Brooke to make the arrangements and transfer Jane Duncan to the ward.

Gill caught her on her way back in to the labour ward. 'Brooke, be an angel and fetch me a delivery pack for the lady in 6, will you? She's looking very hopeful.'

Brooke grabbed the pack and turned to find Jed blocking the doorway, his blue eyes fixed on her face.

'I owe you an apology.'

He looked tired and she wondered whether he'd been called out in the night.

'You don't owe me anything, Jed.' She hugged the delivery pack to her chest, using it as a form of protection, and tried to pass him. She was still terrified he'd press her for more details about Toby and she hadn't decided what to do yet.

'Wait.' He stretched his arm across the doorway to stop her leaving. 'I shouldn't have spoken to you like that but I was just, well, surprised, that's all. After what we shared I thought—' He broke off, his mouth twisted into a wry smile. 'Maybe you're right. Maybe my ego is overdeveloped. I was just shocked that you'd plunged into another relationship so soon.'

She couldn't look at him and her eyes slipped away from his. 'That's OK. You don't need to explain. I need to get this to Gill.'

'How are you getting home tonight?' His voice was a low, masculine growl. 'I'll give you a lift.'

'No.' She shook her head. 'No—I'm fine, really. Forget it, Jed. Please.'

'Brooke, we need to talk.' His voice stroked her senses

and she felt tears clog her throat. She didn't know which was harder to deal with—his coldness or his warmth. Both cut her to the quick because she couldn't do anything about either of them. How could she? She couldn't afford to get close to this man, however strongly she felt about him.

Gill's voice echoed down the corridor. 'Brooke, I need that pack!'

Brooke swallowed and glanced at Jed. 'I've got to go.'

Jed cursed under his breath and raked long fingers through his glossy dark hair. 'We'll talk later.'

'No.' She eased past him and gave him a tired smile. 'There's nothing left to talk about. Let's just leave it now. It's all in the past.'

Without waiting for his reply, she walked quickly to the delivery room, feeling his eyes on her back.

Halfway through the morning she had to call Jed out of his clinic, this time to see a young woman whose blood pressure was worryingly high. She intercepted him in the corridor before he went into the room.

'Sorry to call you...'

He shrugged. 'That's all right. When my senior reg starts, hopefully the load will soon be shared.'

Brooke sincerely hoped so. If she had to keep bumping into Jed this many times a day there was a strong possibility she'd go mad. 'There's a couple of things you ought to know.'

He paused with his hand on the door and lifted an eyebrow. 'About my patient?'

Brooke nodded. 'She's had no antenatal care at all. She hates hospitals and doctors and won't go anywhere near them.'

'Oh, great!' Jed rolled his eyes and sighed. 'This is going to be fun, then. So why is she here?'

'Her boyfriend bullied her into it. They just turned up on the labour ward, demanding treatment for her headache and stomach ache.' Brooke bit her lip.

'Her blood pressure's up in the sky—one-seventy over one-ten—and she's got severe epigastric pain, which she thinks is indigestion, but I think—'

'It's pre-eclampsia,' Jed finished, pulling a face. 'OK. Thanks for the warning. I'll treat her with kid gloves. Do we know why she hates hospitals?'

'No.' Brooke gave him a wry smile and shook her head. 'She hates me too much to tell me.'

'Right.' Jed returned the smile, their differences temporarily forgotten. 'Let's take the bull by the horns, then.'

The woman was openly hostile, refusing to co-operate or communicate in any way. It was left to her boyfriend to give them the information they needed.

Her name was Fiona and at thirty-three years old this was her second pregnancy.

'Have you been seen by a doctor at all in your pregnancy?' Jed's voice was calm and steady but Fiona glared at him.

'No, I haven't. I don't want to be messed with. I just want a natural birth and I knew that if I saw a doctor they'd manage to mess it up in some way. Just like you're about to!'

Jed was silent for a moment. 'How would we mess it up, Fiona?'

'I know what you doctors are like!' Her voice rose hysterically and her hand shook as she tucked a strand of dark hair behind her ear. 'You can't leave things alone. You have to meddle.'

'We don't meddle,' Jed said carefully, 'but sometimes it's necessary to intervene for the good of the baby.'

The pregnant woman swore crudely but Jed didn't react, watching her carefully through narrowed eyes.

'This unit has one of the lowest Caesarean section and forceps rates in the country,' he told her quietly, 'so I can reassure you that we never meddle.'

Fiona glowered at them both. 'You all meddle, given the chance.'

'What are you scared of, Fiona?' He sat down on the edge of the bed, his eyes gentle and sympathetic and his whole manner calm and controlled. 'If you tell me what you're scared of, I can probably help.'

'How?' Fiona's eyes were tormented. 'Can you bring her back?'

'Bring who back?' Jed's eyes never left her face. 'Bring who back?'

Fiona burst into tears and her boyfriend slipped an arm round her shoulders and glared at Jed.

'Now look what you've done. You should be keeping her calm, not winding her up like this!'

'I think it would be better for everyone if you told me exactly what you're afraid of,' Jed said gently, his voice very calm and patient. 'I promise not to do anything to you without your consent, but unless you're straight with me it's impossible for me to reassure you. So can you tell me what happened?'

'My baby died! That's what happened!!' Fiona started to sob hysterically and Brooke felt her heart twist.

'Oh, you poor thing!' She sat down on the bed opposite Jed and tried to take the girl's hand, but it was immediately snatched away.

'She was dead when she was born, and it was the doctors' fault.' Fiona was still sobbing. 'When I got pregnant again I swore I wouldn't go near another hospital and then this happened and he made me come.'

She started to thump her partner who looked totally traumatised.

'Was I wrong to bring her?' He looked at them helplessly and Brooke gave him a sympathetic glance.

'You were absolutely right.'

Jed listened to them all and then shifted his position slightly, his demeanour one of calm confidence. 'OK, Fiona, I want you to listen to me. Are you listening to me?'

Fiona's sobbed lessened slightly and she nodded.

'Right.' Jed's voice was firm and authoritative and it

seemed to work. Fiona calmed down a bit more. 'Where did you have your first baby? Which hospital?'

Fiona told them and Jed nodded to Brooke. 'See if you can get hold of some notes, will you, please?'

Brooke did as he asked and by the time she came back into the room Fiona was much calmer and Jed was still talking, his voice steady and reassuring.

Fiona sniffed. 'So you're saying that if I don't stay in hospital the baby is at risk again.'

'I'm saying exactly that,' Jed agreed, his eyes still fixed on the frightened woman. 'I don't know why your first baby was stillborn because I don't have your hospital records. Sometimes we can't always find a reason.'

'It was their fault—!' Fiona began, and Jed closed strong fingers over the woman's hand.

'For the sake of the baby you're having now, it would be best if you tried not to think about it. The most important thing is to concentrate on what is best for this baby.'

'Is there something wrong with him?' Fiona accepted the tissue that Brooke handed her and blew her nose hard. 'You're telling me he's going to die and it's my fault.'

Jed gave her hand a squeeze. 'I'm not telling you anything of the sort! Your blood pressure is very high and we need to deal with that, but I also need to do is a complete examination. Because you've had no antenatal care at all, I need to find out how pregnant you are and how the baby is. Will you let me do that?'

'Are you a consultant?' Fiona looked at him, her eyes swollen. 'Only I don't want any junior doctors messing around with me. I know they've got to learn but they're not doing it on me.'

'Yes, I'm a consultant. I've been doing obstetrics for twelve years.' Quietly Jed ran through his c.v., giving her details of where he'd trained and the research that he'd done.

'That's the best hospital in the world, isn't it?' Fiona murmured as she listened to what he said. 'So you must know what you're doing.'

'I certainly hope I do.' Jed gave her a gentle smile. 'So now you know more about my credentials than my own mother, will you trust me?'

Fiona bit her lip and gave a brief nod. 'OK.'

'Good.' Jed glanced at Brooke. 'Let's get an ultrasound done and take some blood. I need plasma urate levels and a platelet count, and we need to check her urine again. Now, Fiona, wriggle down the bed so that I can feel the baby. Have you any idea when your last period started?'

'Tenth of July,' Fiona answered promptly, and Jed nodded and moved his hands over her abdomen, barking out more instructions to Brooke and his SHO who had arrived and was hovering expectantly.

'Can you check the EDD, Brooke?'

Fiona scowled. 'Don't use jargon! What's EDD?'

'Expected date of delivery,' Brooke explained gently, checking her calculator. 'And yours is the sixteenth of April.'

'Which would make you about 36 weeks now,' Jed said, rummaging in his pocket and pulling out a tape measure.

'What's that for?' Fiona frowned and Jed gave her a wink.

'It may not look very hi-tech, but it's a surprisingly accurate way of checking how pregnant you are.' He quickly measured from the top of her uterus to her pelvis. 'Now all we need is a scan. Is the baby moving around?'

Fiona patted her stomach and started to look more relaxed. 'All the time.'

'Good. Right. So now let's deal with that blood pressure.'

They spent the rest of the morning sorting Fiona out and by mid-afternoon Jed had decided to try and induce labour.

'You have a condition called pre-eclampsia,' he explained to Fiona, strands of dark hair flopping over his forehead as he spoke. Brooke stared at it for a moment, remembering all too well how it had felt underneath her fingers. 'The only real treatment is to deliver the baby, and as you're already thirty-six weeks pregnant we're going to do exactly that.'

Fiona looked scared. 'You're going to operate?'

'Not yet.' A muscle worked in Jed's jaw and he looked tired. 'I'm going to try and induce your labour first by giving you two pessaries. One now and one in another six hours.'

'OK.' Fiona was clearly putting her faith in Jed and Brooke commented on it as they both sneaked off to the staffroom for a well-deserved cup of coffee, leaving her in Gill's capable hands.

'Yeah, I know. Daunting, isn't it?' He rolled his eyes and gave a shrug. 'Well, better that than have her refuse treatment.'

'She's going to end up with a section,' Brooke said flatly, sipping her coffee and wincing as it burned her mouth. 'Ouch. I wonder what it's like to have a job where you can drink coffee at the right temperature.'

'Don't ask me, I haven't got one,' Jed responded dryly, checking his watch and frowning. 'You might be right about the section but let's see how she goes. She's so nervous I'd rather she laboured if she can. Her clotting times are normal at the moment and we're getting a good reactive heart pattern so we can afford to wait a bit. I need to go down and see a patient on the gynae ward. Bleep me if you need me.'

Brooke stayed with Fiona for the rest of the afternoon and gradually the woman started to thaw, telling her about her first pregnancy and how devastated she'd been when the baby had been stillborn.

It was nearly time for her shift to end when the door opened and Gill put her head round the door.

'Brooke, can I see you?'

Brooke excused herself and followed the sister into the corridor. 'Problems?'

'Sort of. Don't panic, dear, but I've just had a phone call.' Her voice was gentle. 'Your Toby's had a fall at school. He's downstairs in A and E.'

CHAPTER FOUR

HER heart pounding with anxiety, Brooke ignored the lift and sprinted down the stairs to Casualty. Was he badly injured?

'Where is he? I'm looking for Toby Daniels.' Panic showing on her pale face, she grabbed the arm of the first nurse she saw.

'Daniels? He's the little boy who had the teacher with him? They took him to Paediatric Resus,' the girl told her. 'But he's OK, I think. It's not serious.'

Feeling physically sick, Brooke followed the girl through A and E and fought back tears as she saw Toby lying on the trolley.

'Oh, sweetheart!' She rushed forward and stroked his hair, forcing a smile. 'What have you been doing?'

'I fell off the climbing frame,' he mumbled. 'And my head hurts.'

Brooke looked anxiously at the casualty officer but at that moment Jed strode into the room, his expression worried.

'Brooke? Gill told me about your little boy—how is he?'

Jed was here? Why was he here? Another surge of panic hit her but this time for a different reason.

'I don't know.' Her heart was thumping so hard she was aware of every beat. Why did Jed have to turn up now? Taking a deep breath, she concentrated her attentions on the casualty officer. 'What happened?'

'He fell off the climbing frame—from quite high up by all accounts—but he wasn't knocked out and he seems fine, apart from a laceration to his scalp. His teacher was with him a moment ago but she's just nipped off to phone the school. We'll glue the scalp and keep an eye on him for an hour or so.'

Brooke swallowed. 'And then he can go home?'

'Should be able to.' The casualty officer scribbled on the notes. 'I'll give you a head injury form, although if you're medical I don't suppose you need it.'

Toby grinned. 'Can I have another go with your stetha-thingy?'

'Sure, why not?' The doctor handed it over and even obligingly let Toby listen to his chest. 'Toby was telling me his life history. I know that he's nearly six and that he was born prematurely.'

Brooke felt her breathing stop and closed her eyes. Oh, dear God, no. No!

There was a long silence and then Jed cleared his throat. 'You're nearly six, Toby?' His voice sounded strange. 'And you were premature? How premature?'

The little boy wriggled importantly, delighted to be the centre of attention. 'Eight weeks. I had to go in an in-inc— that thing that keeps you warm. What was it called, Mummy?'

'Incubator,' Brooke prompted faintly, not daring to look at Jed. What was going to happen now?

'So when's your birthday Toby?' Jed's voice was hoarse and he wasn't looking at Brooke at all. 'What date?'

'Twentieth of July,' Toby said proudly. 'I'm the next one in my class to have a birthday and I'm going to have a bouncy castle party. Mummy promised.'

'Twentieth of July,' Jed repeated flatly. 'Which means you were due on the twentieth of September, which is forty weeks after the twenty-eighth of December.'

Brooke licked dry lips. 'Jed...'

There was a long silence and the casualty officer glanced curiously from one to the other.

'Is there a problem?'

'No.' Jed's tone was clipped. 'There's no problem.'

Brooke closed her eyes. No problem? There was an enormous problem. And she'd thought her life couldn't get any harder?

'Jed...' What could she say? What could she say to him in front of their child and a strange doctor? Nothing. Her slim shoulders sagged. 'Why don't you come round later?'

His laugh was totally devoid of humour. 'Oh, you can count on it, Brooke. Is your car fixed yet?'

She shook her head. 'No. I took the bus this morning.' Well, two buses, actually.

'Right.' He gave a brief nod, his expression grim. 'I've got to go back to the labour ward to sort out Fiona, but bleep me when you're ready to go home. I'll get someone to cover for me and I'll give you a lift.'

With that he turned on his heel and walked off, leaving her feeling shell-shocked. In the distance she saw him talking to Sean Nicholson, the A and E consultant, and wondered what he was saying. Forcing aside her own problems, she smiled at Toby. First things first. She needed to be there for her son. When he was better she'd have plenty of time to worry about his father.

'This is your car? Really? Wow!' Toby stared at the black sports car in admiration. 'It's great. Can I sit in the front?'

'No, you may not.' Jed gave him an amused look and Brooke wondered how he could seem so relaxed. She was a nervous wreck. But then he glanced at her and the expression in those blue eyes was glacial. He was obviously just making a big effort for Toby's benefit. 'I paid a quick visit to Paediatrics and they've lent me a booster seat so you can hop in the back, young man.'

'Oh.' Toby looked disappointed and then excited again as he scrambled into the back. 'I'm glad I bumped my head.'

'And why's that?' Jed strapped him in, checking that he was securely fastened.

'Because if I hadn't fallen I wouldn't have come to Casualty and I wouldn't have met you and had a ride in this car.'

'Oh, we'd have met, sport.' Jed straightened and his eyes burned into Brooke's, anger and disdain clearly evident. 'It just might have taken a bit longer.'

Brooke swallowed and slid into the passenger seat, heart pounding and limbs shaking. Had she been wrong not to tell him about Toby? Had she made a mistake? For the first time since she'd discovered that she was pregnant she experienced a flicker of doubt, but then she remembered her own childhood and the doubt vanished. No way would she ever want a child of hers to go through what she'd gone through, and if her decision made Jed angry—well, so be it.

Closing her eyes for a minute, she wondered how she was going to weather this latest crisis. Right decision or not, Jed Matthews was a formidable adversary.

By the time Jed pulled up outside the cottage Toby was sound asleep, and he scooped the little boy into his arms and carried him upstairs.

'Where does he sleep?'

'On a mattress in my room at the moment,' Brooke muttered, shrugging out of her coat and draping it over the banister. 'It's his room that has the leak.'

'Right.'

'No, Jed.' Brooke put a hand on his arm, feeling the solid muscle under her fingers. 'I need him close by. I don't want him upstairs.'

He stared at her for a moment, his eyes still cold. 'Brooke, he wasn't knocked out. Sean Nicholson looked at him and reckoned he was fine. I'll give him a quick check over and we'll leave the doors open. We'll hear him if he wakes.'

Brooke swallowed back the lump in her throat. 'I want to be near him...'

Jed's face darkened. 'And I want a conversation without an audience. We have some serious talking to do.'

She sagged against the wall and released his arm. 'I know.'

His face grim, Jed took Toby upstairs and laid him on

the mattress while Brooke fretted next to him. Seeing him so gentle with Toby, it was the very worst kind of torture.

Jed half woke a grumbling Toby and checked him over thoroughly, before tucking the duvet round his sleeping form. 'There, he'll be fine.'

Brooke winced as he gripped her arm firmly and drew her downstairs and into the sitting room.

'Well...' His powerful legs were planted firmly apart and his mouth was set in a grim line. There was no sign of the gentleness he'd shown Toby. He looked formidable, thoroughly male and very, very angry. 'I asked the wrong question, didn't I? I asked you whether Toby was born nine months after our night together.'

She swallowed hard. 'Jed—'

'But he wasn't born nine months after our night together, was he?' His blue eyes glittered dangerously and his tone was acid. 'He was born *seven* months afterwards. I thought you were evasive because you were concealing your relationship with another man, not because you were hiding the fact that we made a child together. So if I'd asked the question a different way, would you have told me the truth? Would you?'

'Jed, please—'

'The truth, Brooke.' His eyes were now cold and unsympathetic. 'I want it now. Straight and with no omissions.'

Brooke twisted her hands together and paced over to the window. It was dark outside with nothing to see, but anything was better than looking at the fury in his eyes.

'Toby is your child.'

Jed gave a short laugh. 'Well, I thought we'd already established that much.'

'Please, please, don't be so angry.' She turned to face him, her eyes huge in her pale face. 'I realise that this is a shock for you, but you have to try and understand—'

'Understand?' His expression was incredulous. 'You were pregnant and never told me and now you expect me to *understand*?'

He was too angry to listen to her and she wrapped her arms around herself in a gesture of self-protection. She didn't know how to get through to him, how to make him listen.

'You were responsible, too, you know!' Her voice was husky and shook slightly. 'It wasn't just me who didn't think of birth control.'

The truth was, neither of them had thought of anything but each other, they'd been so swept away by their feelings.

'I'm not blaming you for the pregnancy.' His voice was hard and he took a steadying breath, obviously still struggling with his temper. 'I'm blaming you for not having contacted me and told me.'

'Why?' Brooke looked at him helplessly. 'We didn't even know each other, Jed. We certainly weren't in a position to bring up a child.'

His eyes flashed angrily and he took a step forward. 'That wasn't your decision to make.'

'It was entirely my decision,' she replied, wondering how her voice could sound so controlled and calm when she was so churned up inside. 'I wasn't a part of your life and you weren't a part of mine.'

'We were a part of each other's lives when we made a child together.' He was brutally frank and not giving an inch. 'I had a right to know that you were pregnant.'

'It wasn't that simple, Jed!'

'Yes, it was.' His expression was grim. 'It was precisely that simple. When you found out that you were pregnant, you should have told me.'

'Well, if you were so bothered why didn't you take precautions?' She glared at him, her dark eyes glittering with unshed tears. What right did he have to judge her so harshly? He wasn't even asking her *why* she hadn't told him. It didn't seem to cross his mind that she might have had a good reason. 'And if you were that bothered, why didn't you try and track me down?'

'You know damn well there was no way I could trace

you. You made sure of that.' He tipped his head back and took a deep breath, struggling to control his temper. 'I tried, believe me. I almost hired a private investigator but then I decided that if you really wanted to hide from me that much I had no right to chase you. And I assumed that if you *were* pregnant you would have found me. You knew where I lived, Brooke.'

She swallowed hard, her heart thumping. He was right, of course. She could have found him. And the truth was she'd been plucking up courage to do just that when she'd discovered she was pregnant. But once she'd found out, there had been no way she could have done it. The pregnancy had ended any hope of a relationship.

'You really wanted to see me again?'

'Was that really so surprising?' Jed gave a derisory laugh and shook his head. 'Maybe it was. I thought that what we had was special. It may have only been one night, but as far as I was concerned it could have been the start of something else. But you didn't want that, did you? You wanted a one-night stand with no strings attached. What was I? Some sort of experiment? Was it just time you lost your virginity?'

She flinched. 'No, of course not.'

'No?' His blue eyes were cold as they raked her pale face. 'Then why didn't you at least wait around to say good morning? Why slink off like a thief in the early hours without leaving so much as a phone number?'

'I told you, I panicked.' She turned to look out of the window again, unable to face the anger in his eyes. 'I'd never done anything like that before—'

'Like what? Slept with a man you didn't know?' His harsh words made her shoulders stiffen and she turned back towards him.

'You were there, too, Jed, remember?' Everything she'd done, he'd done, too. 'You were hardly an innocent bystander. Whatever you may think of me, I behaved in a way that was so totally out of character that night I scared myself. But I don't really expect you to understand that.'

He glared at her, the expression in his blue eyes fierce. 'All right, let's just suppose for one moment that I understand why you left that morning. That still doesn't excuse you from telling me that you were pregnant. Whether you panicked or not, I had a right to know.'

She held his gaze bravely, her heart hammering. 'I can't talk about this with you when you're so angry.'

He tipped his head back and muttered something under his breath. 'Angry? How can you possibly expect me not to be angry?'

'You don't understand—'

'You're dead right, I don't understand.' His icy tone made her wince. 'I don't understand what right you think you had to keep this from me.'

'That's because you won't listen to me. You're so angry you don't want to hear my point of view.' She again wrapped her arms around her slim frame and forced herself to stay calm. She hated it when people were angry. 'Why don't we have this conversation when you've calmed down?'

'Well, forgive me if my control is not what it might be.' His voice was raw and he rubbed long fingers over his brow. 'I've just discovered I've been a father for the past five years so you'll have to excuse me if I'm not in the best of tempers.'

'Jed, what could I have done?' Desperately she appealed to his sense of reason. 'We didn't know each other! I didn't even know your name and you didn't know mine.'

His eyes blazed. 'That's not the point!'

'That's exactly the point,' she said wearily. 'We didn't have a relationship, Jed. We didn't have anything we could build on. Just one night. Hardly a good foundation for child-rearing.'

She knew that better than most.

'So that made it all right, did it? That's how you managed

to justify excluding me from his upbringing.' He was totally unrelenting, so dangerously angry that she turned away from him, but his fingers closed on her arm and he dragged her round to face him. 'What's the matter? Can't you look at me any more? Conscience pricking you, is it, Brooke?'

'No, it isn't!' She jerked her arm away from his grip and rubbed the bruised skin with shaking fingers. 'My conscience is totally clear. I did the best thing for my son.'

'*Our* son, Brooke!' His voice was a low growl. 'Toby is *our* son, and you did not do the best thing for him.'

'That's not fair!' Tears of hurt filled her eyes. 'You're being totally unreasonable!'

'Unreasonable?' Jed's voice was soft and menacing. 'I'm angry because I've discovered that I've been a father for five years and *you think I'm unreasonable*?'

She swallowed at the raw fury in his eyes. 'What I mean is, you're so wrapped up in your own feelings you won't listen to me. I had my reasons—'

'There is nothing—' he said the word with deadly emphasis '—*nothing* you can say that can justify your actions.'

'Jed, please—' Brooke began, but he cut her off, his tone scornful.

'No. You're right.' He closed his eyes briefly and took a deep breath. 'I'm too angry to talk about this now. But you'd better understand one thing. From now on things are going to change.'

Her heart stumbled in her chest and she bit her lip. 'What do you mean? What's going to change?'

'Well, the way Toby's brought up for a start.' His mouth was set in a grim line. 'I've already missed five years of his life. I don't intend to miss any more.'

'He— You—' She swallowed back the lump in her throat. 'I understand that you'll want to see him sometimes—'

'Oh, no, Brooke, not ''sometimes''.' His voice was lethally soft. 'I'm not talking about restricted visitation rights.

Toby is as much mine as yours and I have as much right to be with him as you.'

She blanched. 'You can't want custody of him—'

His anger was unrelenting. 'I don't know what I want yet, but when I decide you'll be the first to know.'

With that he turned on his heel and strode out of her house, slamming the front door behind him.

'How come you've got the headache, Mummy, when I was the one who banged my head?'

Toby finished his cornflakes and watched as his mother swallowed some paracetamol.

'Headaches don't always come from the outside, sweetheart,' she murmured, her dark hair soft and loose around her shoulders. 'Toast?'

He nodded. 'Yes. Shaped like a dinosaur.'

'Please,' she prompted automatically, reaching for a piece of bread and dropping it into the toaster. 'You need to have a quiet day today.'

'Can I watch extra television?' Toby wandered into the sitting room to fetch a toy and bounced back full of excitement. 'Mum, Mum! Jed's coming up the front path. Can I let him in?'

'No!' Brooke put out a hand and pushed him gently back onto his chair, her heart thudding. 'No, darling, you finish your cornflakes. I'll talk to him.'

Tying the belt of her dressing-gown more firmly round her waist and scooping her long hair over one shoulder she tugged open the door, bracing herself for another argument. He hadn't been interested in listening to her side of the story yesterday—why should things be different today?

She swallowed as he leaned against the doorframe, his eyes expressionless as he looked down at her. He was wearing the same clothes he'd had on the previous evening so he'd obviously gone straight back to the hospital, and his hard jaw was darkened by stubble. He looked tough, male and very tired.

'Can I come in?' His voice was gruff and his gaze, although frosty, had lost that glare of anger.

'Why?' She lifted her chin, her attitude defensive. She didn't care if he was tired. She was tired, too. 'So that you can yell at me again?'

'Did I yell?' He leaned one broad shoulder against her doorframe and his dark brows came together in a frown. 'I think you're oversensitive. I may have been angry but I don't remember raising my voice. And if I did you can hardly blame me. It's not every day a man finds out he's—'

'Jed, no!' Brooke covered his mouth with her fingertips, using her eyes to indicate that Toby was just behind them.

'Sorry, didn't think.' His breath brushed the tips of her fingers and she jerked them away as if they'd been scalded as her eyes locked with his. Suddenly her tiny hallway was thrumming with tension.

'What do you want, Jed?' Her voice cracked and her head throbbed. She wasn't up to this, not after the night she'd had. He'd said that he needed to make a decision about what to do. Had he made that decision? Had he come to tell her something? Was he going to try and take Toby from her?

'What do you think? We need to finish our conversation, but clearly this isn't a good time...' his eyes flickered over her shoulders to Toby '...so I'll stick to the practical issues instead.'

Brooke stared at him. 'What practical issues?'

'You need help,' he said bluntly, and she straightened her slim shoulders defensively.

'I don't need help. Toby and I are doing fine...'

He lifted a dark eyebrow. 'Brooke, your car is knackered and your roof has a hole in it. I'll start with the car.'

With that he straightened and walked past her into the kitchen. 'Hello, sport, how's the head?'

He winked at Toby and straddled a kitchen chair, ignoring Brooke who was bristling with outrage but unwilling to say too much in front of her child.

'It hurts a bit but not as much as Mum's,' Toby said sagely, and Jed glanced at Brooke, one dark eyebrow lifting.

'You have a headache?'

'I didn't get much sleep last night,' she said stiffly, and his gaze was cool.

'Conscience bothering you? Why don't you go back to bed for an hour and Toby can give me a hand?'

Toby's eyes were round. 'A hand with what?'

'Mending your mum's car.'

'No way!' Brooke shook her head and put her hands on the soft curve of her hips. 'He's not well enough, Jed—'

'Looks well enough to me,' Jed replied mildly, 'but just to be on the safe side I'll check him over.'

Brooke bit her lip and watched as he withdrew an ophthalmoscope from his jacket pocket.

'Since when did you become an A and E expert?' She knew she sounded grouchy but she couldn't help it.

'Brooke, I'm a doctor. My skills don't end below the navel, you know.' He put a large hand on Toby's forehead and looked in his eyes. 'Look straight ahead, old chap. Good. And again. Great.'

He pocketed the ophthalmoscope and finished examining Toby, who was jumping up and down with excitement.

Jed grinned at him. 'You're fine. So—are you going to help me?'

'Oh, yes, please.' Toby leaped off his chair and scooted round to Jed. 'What do I have to do?'

'Well, you're going to be my assistant and we're going to see if we can fix your car,' Jed told him, his eyes on Brooke who was still seething. 'But don't get your hopes up because from the outside it looks like a lost cause.'

Toby frowned. 'What's a lost cause?'

'I'll explain while we work. Can you hold a screwdriver?' Jed rose in a fluid movement, ignoring Brooke. 'Better put an old coat on or something. You might get dirty.'

'Can I, Mum?' Toby was bursting with excitement. *Please?*

She was cornered. How could she give Jed his marching orders in front of her son? Particularly when Toby was so delighted by the prospect of spending an hour with Jed. How could she deny him that?

'All right.' She smiled at Toby but the smile faded as her eyes lifted to Jed. 'What do you know about cars?'

'Boys with toys, Brooke.' His eyes gleamed mockingly. 'And I'm a surgeon, don't forget. I'm good with the insides of things.'

'Well, if it costs you anything, let me know and I'll pay you back.' Brooke scraped soft dark hair away from her face and blushed as his eyes followed her movement.

He frowned slightly and opened his mouth to say something, but glanced at Toby and clearly thought better of it. 'Why don't we talk about that later? Have you got somewhere I can get changed into something more suitable?'

Brooke watched them go and dragged herself up the stairs to run a bath, her insides knotted with tension. Would Jed say something to Toby? No. Instinctively she knew that, although he was obviously still angry with her, he wouldn't want to upset Toby.

An hour later she was dressed and they were still hunched over the bonnet of her wretched car, Jed's shoulders seeming broader than ever next to Toby's tiny frame. Unobserved, she let her eyes drift hungrily over his hard thighs, the muscle clearly defined by his snug jeans. Leaning her forehead against the window, she watched him, remembering how his body had felt against hers.

Reminding herself that there was no chance of them ever renewing their relationship, she straightened and forced her legs to take her downstairs to the kitchen where she boiled the kettle and pulled some mugs out of the cupboard.

When they still didn't appear she went outside in search of them. This time Jed was lying on his back under the car, those same long, powerful legs stretching onto the pavement as he fiddled.

She cleared her throat. 'I thought you might like some coffee...'

He wriggled out and stared up at her, before sitting up and glancing round for Toby. 'Toby, I need a rag to wipe my hands—could you fetch one for me, please? Good lad.'

Toby sprinted towards the front door and Jed stood up, his face as black as thunder as he looked at Brooke.

'That car is a death trap.' He wiped his damp forehead with his forearm and glared at her. 'It's beyond the skills of any mechanic. It's old and dangerous, Brooke. Crouch down here.'

She blinked at him. 'Why?'

'Just do it, Brooke,' he gritted and she obediently sat down on her heels and stared under the car to where he was pointing. 'See that?'

He poked the screwdriver and a piece of rusty metal snapped away. 'Your chassis is rusted through and that's only a part of it.'

She stiffened defensively. 'I'll ask the garage to look at it.'

He shook his head slowly. 'You don't get it, do you? This car is beyond the help of a mechanic. They'll just charge you to tell you the same thing I have. Have you got a spare set of keys?'

Brooke shook her head. 'No, actually, I—'

'Good.' He locked the car and stuffed the keys into the pocket of his trousers while she watched aghast.

'What do you think you're doing?'

'Preventing you from doing something foolish,' he said grimly. 'That stubborn and independent streak which has helped you to survive for so long is likely to get tangled up with your rebellious streak and land you in trouble. You're not driving this car again, Brooke.'

'Don't you dare dictate what I can and can't do,' she said stiffly 'My life is none of your business.'

'It is when you're driving our son,' he said smoothly. 'Talking of which, he's coming back so smile, will you?'

She took a deep breath and struggled to control her temper. The man was totally overbearing!

'Have we mended it, Jed?' Toby looked anxious and Jed gave his shoulder a squeeze.

'You did a great job but I've had a better plan.'

'What?'

'It's a secret. You'll find out later.' Jed gave him a wink and then his eyes narrowed. 'Toby, who looks after you when your mum goes out?'

Toby looked puzzled. 'Mary looks after me before and after school.'

'What about if Mummy goes out with friends?'

Toby's face cleared. 'You mean like Suzie?'

Jed's eyes flickered to Brooke. 'Yes—like Suzie.'

'Well, Mary sometimes comes or Harriet from next door.'

'Could Harriet look after you this evening for a few hours? I'd like to take your mum out to dinner.'

'I'll go and ask her!' Before Brooke could stop him, Toby was sprinting up Harriet's path.

'What do you think you're doing?' She turned on Jed, her dark eyes blazing with anger. 'You can't just barge in here and dictate my life! My car is none of your business, Jed, and my son is none of your business either. And I will not have dinner with you.'

'*Our* son, Brooke.' He emphasised the word carefully, his voice soft. 'You keep making that mistake. Toby isn't just your son. He's *our* son. And he certainly is my business and so is everything that involves him, including that death trap that you loosely call a car. And you are having dinner with me tonight.'

She glared at him. 'Or what?'

'Or we continue the conversation here.' His tone was hard. 'It's your choice.'

'Some choice! I can be yelled at here or somewhere else. What difference will it make, being in a restaurant?' she asked bitterly, wrapping her arms round her waist.

'Well, I can't strangle you in a public place for a start.'

He picked up the jacket he'd slung over the roof of the car and turned to face her, his legs planted firmly apart. 'I'm not trying to take over, Brooke. I can see how independent you are and I respect that. I can't say I understand it because I would have thought you would have been grateful for help, but I do respect it. But we still need to talk and neutral territory might be a good idea.'

'You wouldn't listen to me yesterday...'

He gave a sigh and raked long fingers through his dark hair. 'I know I wouldn't, and I'm sorry about that. But in the circumstances you can hardly blame me. I assure you that tonight I'll listen.'

She hesitated, the anxiety building inside her. 'Have you decided what you want to do?'

'We can't talk about it now.' Jed's eyes slipped warningly to the neighbours' front path. 'He's coming back.'

Which meant she had to wait all day to find out if he was going to try and take her child away from her. Her head throbbed and she rubbed her temples with shaking fingers, forcing a smile as Toby came skipping back down the path, excitement all over his face.

'Harriet says yes.'

'Great.' Jed squeezed the boy's shoulder with a gentle hand and glanced at Brooke. 'Any chance of that coffee now?'

Did she have any choice? Marching back into the house, Brooke made coffee and handed him a mug with as much grace as she could muster.

'That smells good. I don't think I got a single thing to eat or drink last night.' He sniffed appreciatively and settled himself on one of the kitchen chairs, grinning at Toby who padded into the room with an armful of plastic dinosaurs.

'These are all mine.' Toby let them all tumble onto the kitchen table and Jed blinked in amazement.

'That's quite a collection. Which one's your favourite?'

'My giant triceratops.' Toby handed it to him solemnly and Jed inspected it carefully, his handsome face serious.

'He's great. I didn't have anything like this when I was your age. Where did he come from?'

'Mummy bought him for me.' Toby beamed and Jed glanced towards her, an odd expression on his face.

His scrutiny made her uncomfortable and she scrabbled around in her brain for something neutral to talk about.

'So—did you have a busy night?' Brooke knew her voice sounded stilted but she couldn't help that. Maybe if they talked about work they might be able to temporarily shelve their differences. 'What happened to Fiona?'

'Yes, I was very busy—courtesy of having no junior staff—and Fiona was part of the reason.' Jed dutifully examined each dinosaur in turn, lining them up on the table until there was barely room for the coffee-mugs.

Brooke poured Toby a glass of milk and handed it to him. 'You had to section her?'

'As you predicted.' He rubbed his eyes and smothered a yawn, taking the last dinosaur from Toby. 'Ah, I recognise that one. Tyrannosaurus. Scary meat-eater.'

Brooke leaned against the fridge and watched him. 'So what happened with her?'

He shrugged. 'Her platelets dropped and that was that really. We had to get the baby out, particularly with her history.'

Brooke pulled a face. 'I bet she was stressed.'

'Actually, she wasn't that bad.' He took a mouthful of coffee. 'I think by the time I had to break the news to her about the section she'd already had time to get used to being in hospital and she'd started to trust us.'

'And was the baby OK?'

'Gorgeous. Bouncing boy. They were thrilled.' He smiled at the memory and her heart did a strange flip. No wonder she'd behaved so rashly with him—what woman wouldn't?

'I'm pleased.'

'Yes—it was a good outcome.' He rubbed the bridge of his nose with long fingers, clearly tired. 'And then, to add to the workload, Jane Duncan decided that she wasn't going to hang onto that baby any longer and I ended up sectioning her, too.'

Brooke frowned. 'How many weeks was she? Thirty-three? How's that baby?'

'In Special Care, but doing all right, according to Sita,' Jed told her, subduing a massive yawn. 'I'd better go and get some sleep. I've managed to persuade Robert Peters to cover for me so I'm off until tomorrow morning.'

'You're going home?' She realised suddenly that she didn't even know where he lived. 'Have you rented somewhere round here?'

'I have a house.' He finished his coffee and put the mug down on the table. 'I had it built years ago as an investment but I let it out as holiday accommodation until the end of last year.'

'You've had a house here for years?' She frowned and shook her head. 'I don't understand. Do you come from round here, then?'

'I was born and brought up just down the road in Grasmere,' he told her, leaning back in his chair and stretching his long legs in front of him. 'My parents still live there and my older brother is close by, too.'

'I didn't realise...' She put her coffee down, untouched. 'And that's how you know Sean Nicholson?'

'We were at school together. Never thought Sean would settle down but he's married now with two children and another one on the way.' His long fingers played with the mug of coffee as he watched her. 'Funny how life turns out.'

His cold blue gaze was accusing again and she turned away and tipped her coffee down the sink. She felt too sick to drink it.

'Shall we play a game with my dinosaurs now?' Suddenly bored by adult conversation, Toby wriggled on his chair and looked for a distraction. 'You can be the plant-eaters and I'll be the meat-eaters.'

'That sounds like a slightly mismatched contest,' Jed

drawled gently, ruffling the boy's hair and giving him an affectionate look that twisted Brooke's insides.

'Jed has to leave now, sweetheart,' Brooke said gruffly, 'but I'm sure he'd like to play with your dinosaurs another time.'

'You're right. I certainly would.' He rose to his feet and picked up his jacket and car keys. 'I'll pick you up at seven-thirty.'

CHAPTER FIVE

JED took Brooke to a small pub tucked away on the edge of a village. It was warm and welcoming and full of locals, and Jed grabbed a small table tucked in one corner, close to the flickering fire.

'It's not pretentious but the food's good,' he said gruffly, shrugging off his coat and pulling out a chair for her. 'I thought it was more informal than a restaurant.'

'It's fine,' Brooke said stiffly, sitting down and picking up a menu without enthusiasm. She didn't care where she was and she certainly didn't feel hungry. Her head still throbbed—probably the anticipation of yet more confrontation, she thought wearily.

Jed ordered for both of them and settled himself more comfortably in his chair, his blue eyes fixed on her face.

'OK. I've calmed down and I'm ready to listen.'

'Listen to what?'

'To what you have to say. You said there were reasons for not having told me about Toby.' His voice was low and very male. 'I'd like to hear them, Brooke.'

She stared into the fire, the heat and the flames almost hypnotic. 'You wouldn't understand.'

'Try me.'

There was a long silence and she took a sip of her drink. 'I wasn't meant to be there that night.'

'At the ball?'

'That's right.' She put her drink back on the table and stared into the fire again. 'I never went out. I was too busy studying, and when I wasn't studying I was working.'

'Working? You had a second job?' His voice was sharp. 'Doing what?'

'I was a waitress in a bistro.'

'Why did you have to do that?'

She gave him an impatient look. 'Because we needed the money—why do you think?'

'Who needed the money?' He frowned. 'Who were you living with?'

She picked up her glass and took a sip. 'My father.'

'Your father encouraged you to hold down two jobs?' Jed looked stunned and she shifted in her seat.

'It was more complicated than that, Jed.'

'I'm still listening.'

She glanced at him and sighed. He wasn't going to let her get away with anything less than the full story. Oh, well, why not? What difference did it make if he knew the truth? At least he might begin to understand her reasons for not telling him about Toby.

'My parents didn't plan to have me,' she began, fiddling with her glass and staring at the fire. She didn't look at him but she could feel his eyes fixed on her. 'I was an accident. My mum was young and, well, anyway, they got carried away and I was the result. Without me they never would have got married.' She took a deep breath. 'And that's why I couldn't tell you that I was pregnant. I didn't want to put you in the same position that my father was in when he made my mother pregnant.'

There was a long silence while Jed considered her words and then he spoke, his voice low and gruff. 'How do you know they wouldn't have got married anyway?'

'Because my father told me. Repeatedly.' Brooke took a sip of her drink, her hands shaking slightly. 'He told me that if it hadn't been for me he never would have settled down so young and would have developed his career instead. Because of me he was forced to take a different sort of job and he was never happy.'

'Wait a minute.' Jed lifted a hand to interrupt her, his expression incredulous. 'You're telling me that your father blamed you for his poor career decisions?'

She swallowed. 'Well, yes. I was the reason he made those decisions. If my mother hadn't been pregnant he would have done something entirely different with his life.'

Jed muttered something under his breath and then leaned back in his seat, his face grim. 'Go on.'

Brooke hesitated, her dark eyes wary. 'Y-you're angry again and you said you wouldn't be angry tonight.'

He took a deep breath and gave her a brief smile. 'I'm not angry—at least, not with you. Tell me the rest of the story. What about your mother? Couldn't she get a job?'

'She was ill.' Brooke fiddled with her glass again. 'And that was my fault, too.'

'This I must hear.' Jed sat back in his chair and shook his head slowly, his expression one of disbelief. 'Go on. Enlighten me. What was wrong with her and how was that your fault?'

'She had postnatal depression,' Brooke said flatly, not looking at him. She didn't want to look at him. Didn't want to know if he was sympathetic or not. She didn't want sympathy. She just wanted to tell her story and go home. 'And naturally my father blamed me for that, too.'

'But postnatal depression can be treated.' Jed was clearly baffled, and she shook her head impatiently.

'We're talking twenty-six years ago, Jed. No one recognised it for what it was. My mum became housebound, emotionally crippled, unable to do anything for herself or anyone else. My dad had to care for her. He lost his job. The marriage was a disaster. It was all my fault.'

'Brooke—'

'Let me finish.' She risked a glance at him but his expression was unreadable. 'I took a second job and gave Dad as much money as I could. I never went out because I was too tired and too busy working.'

'But you went to the ball.'

She gave a short laugh. 'Yes. For one night I pretended to be someone I wasn't, so maybe your Cinderella analogy wasn't so far out. I was a student nurse and one of the doctors felt sorry for me and gave me a ticket. I sneaked in like a child at a grown-ups' party, feeling totally out of place.'

'You didn't look out of place.' His voice was gruff and he took a mouthful of frothy beer. 'You looked stunning.'

The unexpected compliment made her blush and she dipped her head, her dark hair tumbling over her face. 'And then I met you. Apart from mild flirtations at the bistro, I'd never really had anything to do with men before. Meeting you was—' She broke off, not sure just how honest to be and he prompted her gently.

'Was what?'

She hesitated, her colour deepening and he prompted her again.

'Meeting me was what? I want honesty, Brooke. Tell me how you felt.'

She bit her lip. He wanted honesty. She might as well give it to him.

'It was the most exciting thing that had ever happened to me.' She spoke the words so softly that she wondered whether he'd heard her, but the look in his eyes told her that he had. She held his gaze bravely. 'You were so good-looking, so self-assured and strong—I'd never met anyone like you before. I was totally intoxicated.'

Jed gave a groan and closed his eyes briefly. 'And I took advantage of you.'

'No.' She gave him a wan smile. 'No, not that. I wanted you so badly I would have seduced you if necessary. I don't know what happened to me that night, but I was with you all the way, Jed.'

She broke off as their food arrived and then picked up her fork without much enthusiasm. 'You didn't take advantage of me, but I'd never felt that way or behaved that way before, and when I woke up in your bed, in your arms...I panicked.'

'I can imagine.' For once there was no sarcasm in his voice and she risked a glance. His blue eyes locked with hers and he shook his head slowly. 'What an awful childhood you must have had.'

She pushed her food around her plate. 'I— Do you understand now why I couldn't tell you about Toby?'

'Yes.' He nodded slowly. 'I understand why you thought you were doing the right thing. But you could have trusted me, you know.'

She swallowed. 'No. It was just one night, Jed. I didn't really know you and you didn't know me. Neither of us meant that to happen—'

'I know that, and it was my responsibility, but I wanted you so badly...' He sat back with a groan and closed his eyes briefly. 'I was selfish and I'm sorry, Brooke.'

'Selfish?' Her eyes widened. 'How were you selfish? You didn't do anything wrong.'

'How can you say that?' He made an impatient sound and raked long fingers through his glossy dark hair, his expression incredulous. 'I made you pregnant that night.'

'Neither of us was thinking straight. We were both carried away—'

'I shouldn't have been.' His blue eyes searched hers and he shook his head slowly. 'You must have hated me when you found out. How can you be so forgiving?'

'What is there to forgive, Jed? And I certainly didn't hate you. How could I hate you?' Her brief glance was shy, almost embarrassed. If he knew what she really felt about him, he'd collapse on the spot. 'That night was so special... I certainly didn't hate you.'

'And then you made a new life for yourself and I turned up with no warning and started yelling at you without listening to your side of the story.' He swore under his breath and rubbed his temples with strong fingers. 'What a louse! I'm sorry, Brooke.'

'You didn't yell,' she reminded him with a trace of humour in her voice. 'I have it on good authority that you didn't yell.'

He shook his head and sat back in his chair. 'How can

you joke about it? You should want to throw something at me.'

'You're rather a lot bigger than me, so that probably wouldn't be wise.' She nibbled a chip and gave him a wary smile. Maybe it would be all right. He'd certainly calmed down.

He was watching her closely, his handsome face serious. 'I'd never done that before either, you know.'

'Done what?'

'Got so carried away that I forgot to protect the woman I was with.' His voice was low but she blushed deeply and cast an anxious look towards the bar but no one was listening.

'It doesn't matter Jed.'

'It matters a great deal,' he said dryly, picking up his fork and starting to eat. 'When I woke up the next morning and found you gone I couldn't believe it. I consoled myself with the fact that if you were pregnant then you'd find me. I feel hideously guilty that you've had to struggle on your own for all these years. How did you manage?'

'I didn't find out I was pregnant for two months.' She picked at her food, the warmth from the fire comforting. 'When I did—well, you can imagine that my father was less than pleased. All my life he'd drummed into me that an unplanned pregnancy is the worst thing that can happen to anybody. That having responsibility for me had ruined his life. When he thought he was going to have responsibility for a grandchild too, he nearly had a stroke!'

Jed's jaw was tense. 'I wish you'd contacted me—'

'You still don't get it, do you?' She put down her fork and shook her head slowly. 'For twenty years I was a total burden to someone. Because of me they got married when they were totally unsuited. I wasn't really wanted or loved, I was just tolerated. I was someone's responsibility. Something to be shouldered as a penance for a mistake. There was no way on this earth I would ever inflict that same situation on my own child.'

Jed's mouth tightened and his blue eyes hardened. 'Don't ever compare me to your father.'

'But the situation was the same, can't you understand that?' She was desperate to make him understand, to make him see why she had never told him about Toby. 'You would have been taking on a responsibility which wasn't of your choosing, something that would have affected your whole life and your career.'

He leaned forward, his blue eyes intense. 'But that should have been my decision to make, Brooke.'

She shook her head sadly. 'No. Because you're a thoroughly decent man, Jed—I knew that from the first moment I met you. You would have done something stupid, like offering to marry me, and it would have been for all the wrong reasons. That's the sort of relationship I've had all my life and I deserve more than that and so do you. And that's why I never told you.'

Jed was silent for a moment, digesting what she'd said. 'So what did you do? Did your father come good in the end?'

'No.' Brooke's tone was flat and she didn't elaborate. 'I carried on working, and once the baby was born I used childminders. Eventually I qualified and did my midwifery, but London was too expensive and I always loved the mountains so I moved here.'

'But what about your mother?' He obviously couldn't believe what he was hearing. 'Didn't she support you?'

'My mother died when I was eleven.' Brooke's voice was husky as she pushed the food around her plate. 'She was hit by a car and no one ever really knew whether it was an accident or suicide.'

There was a long silence and then he spoke, his voice soft. 'I'm so sorry.'

'Don't be.' She gave a weary smile. 'It was awful but it was a long time ago.'

'I can't begin to imagine how you must have struggled.

How on earth did you bring up a child on a nurse's salary?' He sounded incredulous and her eyes gleamed with humour.

'You make it sound as though I'm on the breadline! It's not that bad, Jed.'

'But it's bad enough, isn't it? Hence the heating, roof and car,' he murmured, clearly ticking them off in his mind. 'You're so stretched financially that every time something goes wrong it's a major problem for you. Am I right?'

She stiffened and dropped her fork onto her plate. 'My finances are none of your business!'

'On the contrary, they're entirely my business. You've been supporting our child on your own for five years. I owe you money.'

Brooke bristled at his words. 'You don't owe me anything! I don't want your money.'

'Brooke, Toby is *our* child.' The words were gentle but firm. 'He's my responsibility as well.'

Brooke shook her head, her heart pounding. She couldn't believe she was hearing this. 'Haven't you heard a word I've said? Toby isn't going to be anyone's responsibility.'

'What about you? He was landed on you,' Jed said bluntly, but she gave a soft smile.

'No. Toby was a gift to me.' Her eyes misted. 'A precious gift.'

'A precious gift?' He looked at her curiously and shook his head. 'He turned your whole life upside down.'

'He was the best thing that ever happened to me.'

His eyes searched hers as if he was trying to read her mind. 'Tell me something else. I realise now why you were so keen to pretend you didn't know me and keep me at a distance. If Toby hadn't blown your cover, would you have told me eventually?'

'I don't know,' she said honestly, resisting the temptation to lean on that broad chest and cry her eyes out. He wasn't hers to cry on. 'Probably not. What was the point in telling you? So that we could be a drain on your resources? I wouldn't do that to you, Jed.'

'A drain on my resources?' He blinked at her and looked baffled. 'Brooke, you don't know anything about my resources but, believe me, it would take quite a bit to drain them. I have every intention of helping you out financially.'

'I don't want your money! I've already told you that.'

He cleared his plate and sat back in his chair, his blue eyes narrowed. 'Calm down. I do understand why you feel like that—I'm not that insensitive. I totally understand the reason you're so fiercely independent and the reason you don't want to accept help. But I'm not your father. I don't resent helping with the upkeep of our child. I will never make him feel guilty or beholden to me.'

'But you didn't choose to have him—'

'No,' he said honestly, 'but that doesn't mean I resent him. I think he's great, if you must know, and I love him already. You've done a good job, Brooke.'

Brooke looked away so that he wouldn't see her eyes mist. This was so hard. He was such a thoroughly decent man, so strong and dependable, with none of the weaknesses her father had shown. This man would never blame anyone else for his failings, not that Jed seemed to have many...

'So, tell me about you.' She fiddled with her glass, her dark hair spilling over her shoulders. 'What do your parents do?'

'They dabble in all sorts of things,' he said with a brief smile. 'My dad is actually a vet but my older brother, Phil, runs a property company and we all have a hand in it, Mum included. Keeps us out of mischief and it's a welcome distraction from medicine.'

'You mentioned another brother...'

He nodded. 'Tom. He's a surgical registrar in London, but he's dying to get back up here. We all hate the city really but he wants to finish his surgical rotation and then he'll look for a job here.'

'Like you did?'

He smiled. 'Something like that, although don't get the

impression we live in each other's pockets because we don't.'

She swallowed. 'But you're close.'

'Yes.' His eyes were suddenly gentle. 'And I know how lucky that makes me.'

'When we met that night—' she looked at him curiously, suddenly anxious to fill in the gaps in her knowledge '—where were you working? What were you doing?'

'I was a registrar in obs and gynae. I stayed in London as a senior reg and then I got this post.' He drained his glass and gave her a smile. 'It's a good unit.'

'I know.' She gave him a shy smile. 'We were all afraid that the new consultant would be the sort who interfered with every labour. You know, out with the forceps at the slightest hint of a problem.'

'Not me,' he drawled, his eyes dancing. 'I'm too lazy for that. If a woman can do it by herself I'd much rather save myself the work.'

But she knew that wasn't true. He wasn't lazy at all. Just incredibly gifted, and forward-thinking. Ahead of many of his profession. But talking about work wasn't why they were in the pub.

She stirred herself. 'So, have you decided what you want to do?' Her voice was gruff and she rubbed damp hands on her soft wool skirt as she waited for his answer.

'Not yet. Look at me, Brooke.' His tone was insistent and she lifted her eyes.

'What?'

'You're overlooking one thing in all this. What we shared that night was very special—we both felt it.'

Her heart stumbled in her chest. 'It was just one night, Jed—'

'But it doesn't have to be.' The expression in his eyes made her stomach flip over and her pulse race.

'What are you suggesting?'

'We could get to know each other better and see what happens.'

Her eyes widened and she shook her head violently. 'No! It wouldn't work. It just wouldn't work.'

'Give me one good reason.'

'I can give you a very good reason,' she said quietly, her voice sad. 'Toby. I know you love him already and you'll be a great father. And no matter what you truly feel about me, you'll try and make it work for Toby's sake.'

'No—'

'Yes,' she said firmly, 'can't you understand that, Jed? We can be friends and we should be for Toby, but we can never be anything more because that would just be satisfying your sense of responsibility.'

He swore softly and shook his head in frustration. 'Do you really have such a low opinion of yourself?'

'I'm a realist,' she said simply. 'The only reason you want a relationship with me is because you feel a responsibility towards Toby.'

A muscle worked in his hard jaw. 'So if I can prove you wrong about that...'

'You can't.' She finished her drink and stood up. 'Shall we call it a night?'

He gave a short laugh. 'It's just as well we decided on the pub. If we'd been at home now I definitely would have just strangled you. Brooke...' He put his hands on her shoulders and turned her to face him. 'You owe it to Toby to give it a try.'

'Don't tell me what I owe my son, Jed.' She shrugged his hands away and her gaze was cool as she slipped her arms into her warm jacket. 'I know better than you what it's like to have parents who aren't in love but are obsessed with responsibility. Believe me, it doesn't do much for a child's confidence or happiness. If we got together, sooner or later you'd end up resenting me and feeling frustrated by all the things that marriage to me had made you miss out on. I don't want that for Toby.'

Neither did she want it for herself. She couldn't live with a man she was crazy about, knowing that he didn't love her.

* * *

The next morning Jed turned up in time to drop Toby at the childminder's and give her a lift to work.

'This is ridiculous,' Brooke muttered as she slipped into the passenger seat. 'You can't provide a taxi service every day. We could have caught the bus.'

She'd already looked in the paper for cars, but hadn't seen anything within her price range that looked reasonable.

'It's pouring with rain again.' He swung the car onto the main road and put his foot down, much to Toby's delight. 'I thought you'd be pleased.'

Actually, she was. The weather was grim and if she was honest she'd been dreading battling her way to work on the bus.

She relaxed slightly, although there was something in Jed's face that made her feel uneasy. After her final outburst the previous evening he hadn't really said anything. He'd just driven her home in silence and left her with a promise to collect them both in the morning.

What was he up to?

Before she could give it any more thought they'd dropped Toby and arrived at the hospital.

'I hope no one sees us,' she mumbled as she released her seat belt and reached forward to open the door.

'Ashamed of me, Brooke?' He sounded amused and she gave him a wry look. Hardly. There wasn't a woman alive who'd be ashamed of being seen with Jed Matthews.

'I just don't like gossip.'

'Ignore it,' he advised, switching off the engine and reaching for his briefcase. 'I've got a ward round in five minutes so I've got to dash. I'll catch up with you later.'

With that he strode across the car park, leaving her staring after him.

The day was as busy as usual, and halfway through the morning there was great excitement because Ally Nicholson, wife of the A and E consultant, went into labour.

'It was far too early to come in,' she grumbled as Brooke made her comfortable in one of the special labour rooms.

'But Sean is like a cat on hot bricks. This is the second time we've been through this but he's just as bad this time round.'

'It always happens with doctors.' Brooke laughed, checking Ally's temperature and blood pressure. 'I suppose they know too much. Where is he now?'

'Dropping the other two off with my mum.' Ally screwed up her face as another pain hit her. 'Ouch! I tell you, I wish it was Sean that was having it. He's much tougher than me.'

'Not that tough,' drawled a voice from the doorway, and Sean Nicholson walked in, his dark eyes worried. 'Are you doing all right, babe?'

'I'm fine.' Ally rolled her eyes and curled her fingers into the bedspread. 'I think I might be further on than I thought. These pains are pretty bad and pretty close together.'

Brooke moved the CTG machine closer to the bed. 'Well, I'll just attach you to this for a minute and then I'll examine you.'

Sean paced over to the window and back again. 'Is Jed around? I think you should see a doctor.'

'Sean!' Ally shook her head and gave him an outraged look. 'Calm down, will you? I don't need Jed. This is going to be a perfectly normal delivery. I want a midwife.'

Sean took a deep breath and threw Brooke an apologetic look. 'I wasn't questioning your skills—'

'It's fine, Dr Nicholson,' she said quietly. 'I understand your concerns. If there's anything at all untoward, please, rest assured that I'll call Jed.'

She wasn't offended. Most doctors were nervous wrecks when their wives were in labour.

'Call me Sean, please.' He sank into a chair next to the bed and closed his eyes. 'Did you have to do this today, Ally? I was up all night with a motorcyclist who had an argument with a lorry.'

'Well, I'm sorry to inconvenience you,' Ally shot back tartly, but Brooke could see from the way they exchanged glances that they were crazy about each other. What was it like to have that sort of relationship with the man you'd married? She swallowed hard and concentrated on the trace and then examined Ally.

'Eight centimetres,' she murmured a few minutes later, dropping her gloves in the bin and scribbling on the chart. 'It won't be long at all, Ally.'

'Thank goodness for that.' Sean raked a hand through his cropped dark hair. 'I can't stand the strain.'

'*You* can't stand the strain?' Ally thumped him playfully and then moaned and grabbed his hand. 'Oh, Sean!'

'It's OK, sweetheart, I'm here.' His voice was gruff and he looked helplessly at Brooke. 'Are you sure she doesn't need a section?'

'Calm down, Nicholson.' Jed's lazy drawl made them all glance up and he grinned at them. 'Everything OK here?'

'It's fine,' Brooke and Ally chorused, but Sean shook his head.

'No, it's not fine. How you can deal with this every day, I don't know. You must have nerves of steel, Matthews!'

Jed laughed and picked up Ally's notes. 'She's not my wife, Sean. It makes a difference, believe me.'

For a brief moment his eyes rested on Brooke and then he swivelled his gaze to Ally.

'How are you doing?'

'Fine.' Ally gave a grunt and breathed in sharply as another pain hit her. 'But, for goodness' sake, tell this brute I don't need a section, will you?'

Jed laughed. 'You heard the woman, Sean. She doesn't need a section.'

Sean groaned and rubbed his forehead with his fingers. 'You wait, Matthews. One day you'll be in this position and you'll understand the appeal of surgery. Clean, fast and predictable.'

'And totally unnecessary,' Jed replied calmly. 'She was fine last time, Sean. There's no reason to suspect she'll be anything but fine this time. Brooke's a fantastic midwife. You couldn't do better.'

Brooke felt her face warm at the compliment and busied

herself, preparing for the delivery, but she knew Ally was watching her curiously.

Jed stayed for a few more minutes and then left, promising to pop back in 'just to be nosy' before Ally delivered.

Brooke grabbed a quick lunch and then went back to Ally who was pacing the floor with Sean's help. Brooke turned the lights down in the delivery room and put on some soft music.

'You're doing so well, Ally.' Apart from gas and air, Sean's wife had managed without any pain relief.

Ally eased herself back onto the bed and sank against the cushions. 'I'd forgotten how agonising it is.' She was breathless and her face was white with strain. 'I think I want to push.'

Brooke snapped on a pair of gloves. 'Just hold on a second while I examine you quickly. I don't want you pushing if you're not fully dilated.'

She knew from the notes that Ally was a GP, but experience had taught her that a woman in labour still wanted explanations, no matter how professionally qualified they were.

'I feel sick,' Ally mumbled, and retched weakly into the bowl that Brooke quickly produced.

'You're doing fine, sweetheart,' Sean murmured, stroking his wife's blonde hair gently. His dark eyes were strained as he looked at Brooke. 'How long now?'

'Not long.' Brooke glanced up as the door opened and Jed entered.

'How are you doing here?'

'The head's down and she's ready to push,' Brooke murmured, encouraging Ally gently as she gave a groan. 'I need another midwife—can you call for someone, Jed?'

'I want to kneel.' Ally struggled and Brooke helped her, but Sean was aghast.

'You can't kneel, Ally! They won't be able to deliver it like that.'

'Shut up, Nicholson,' Jed muttered, taking his shoulder

and drawing him away slightly. 'Leave Brooke to it, will you? The midwives in this unit can deliver mothers hanging from the ceiling if that's what they want.'

'I don't want to hang from the ceiling,' Ally joked, and then groaned again as another pain hit her.

Grateful for Jed's presence, Brooke talked quietly to Ally and together they found the position that she was most comfortable in. Suzie slipped into the room quietly and opened up the delivery pack.

Ally groaned. 'Can I push?'

'Whenever you like.' Brooke knew that the baby was going to be delivered quite quickly and got herself ready, kneeling on the bed with Ally. Thank goodness for the loose cotton trousers they all wore as part of their uniform. Much more practical than a short dress! 'Stop pushing when I say, Ally. OK, pant now. Pant. Well done.'

The head was delivered without any fuss and quickly Brooke checked that the cord wasn't round the baby's neck.

Sean was stroking his wife's head now, murmuring words of encouragement in his deep voice.

Ally clutched the back of the bed and gasped as another pain hit her. Brooke delivered the shoulders and then the rest of the baby slithered into her waiting hands with an outraged yell.

'Little boy,' Brooke told them with a smile, waiting for Sean and Suzie to settle Ally before handing her the new baby.

'Oh, Sean!' Ally burst into tears and Sean blinked a few times and kissed his wife on the mouth.

'Clever thing.'

Jed grinned and leaned over to take a peep. 'Doesn't look a bit like you, Nicholson, so he should do all right in life.'

Sean laughed, the relief evident on his face. 'I'm sorry I was so stressed—'

'You? Stressed?' Jed's firm mouth twitched and he glanced at Brooke. 'We didn't notice, did we?'

'Hardly at all.' Brooke laughed, concentrating her attention on clamping the cord and delivering the placenta.

Half an hour later Jed was long gone and Ally was spruced up and happily feeding her new son.

'He's starving,' she murmured, stroking the downy head with a gentle hand.

'He's not the only one.' Sean dropped a kiss on her forehead. 'Can you do without me if I go and grab a sandwich?'

'Oh, we'll cope,' Ally said, her eyes laughing as she glanced at her husband.

'Use the staffroom,' Brooke offered, her smile slightly shy. There was something very daunting about Sean Nicholson.

'Poor man.' Ally chuckled and settled herself more comfortably. 'He could never have been an obstetrician. He'd have had the highest section rate in Britain.'

'I've heard he's an incredibly skilled trauma doctor.' Brooke was clearing up quietly and chatting at the same time.

'He is.' Ally's face glowed with pride and love. 'And surprisingly enough he's incredibly calm in a crisis. Not that you'd think it from seeing him in the delivery room! He was the same with our other one.'

'I thought you said you have three children?'

'We have, but our first is adopted. She was my sister's child,' Ally told her, switching the baby to the other breast with all the skill of the seasoned breast-feeder. 'Then I met Sean and we had Katy. She's two now and into everything.'

They chatted for a while longer and Ally looked at her curiously.

'So what's with you and Cumbria's most eligible bachelor?'

Brooke concentrated on clearing up. 'Who's that, then?'

'Oh, come on!' Ally grinned. 'There's so much electricity coming from you and Jed I thought my hair would stand on end.'

'You're imagining things.' Brooke blushed and tossed a pile of debris into the bin. 'It's nothing.'

'Nothing, eh?' Ally's blue eyes teased her gently. 'Well, if a man looks at you like that when it's "nothing", goodness knows how he looks when he means it.'

Had Jed been looking at her?

'You must be an amazing woman,' Ally drawled, cuddling the baby closer. 'Women have been trying to hook Jed since he was in nappies, according to Sean.'

'I haven't hooked him,' Brooke said gruffly, and Ally grinned.

'Well, if you haven't then you're daft. It's not often these days you find a rich, good-looking man who hasn't already been snapped up.'

Suddenly Brooke remembered Jed's comment about his financial resources not being easy to drain, and wondered just how rich he was.

Ally's smile faded. 'I hope I haven't offended you, but the way he was looking at you made me assume...'

Brooke gave her a stiff smile. 'There's nothing between Jed and me. Nothing at all.'

Ally looked at her sagely. 'Right. I see.'

Brooke bit her lip but fortunately at that moment Sean returned, looking considerably revived. They both thanked her warmly as she arranged for Ally to be transferred to the ward.

Gill popped her head round the door as she was restocking the room. 'Delivery for you in my office. You have to sign for it.'

Sign for what?

Frowning slightly, she followed Gill up the corridor and into the office. A man was standing by the window.

'Are you Brooke Daniels?'

She nodded. 'Yes.'

'I've got a delivery for you. You need to sign for it, please.'

Brooke stared at him, puzzled. 'But I'm not expecting anything.'

He held out a board and a set of keys. 'If you could sign in the two places I've marked, please, Miss Daniels.'

Brooke signed and stared at the keys blankly. What was going on?

'It's parked in the second row,' the man told her, tearing off the top sheet and handing it to her. 'Hope you like the colour. The man thought red would be best.'

'Best for what?'

'Your new car.' The man looked at her face and shook his head with a smile. 'You mean you didn't know? Pretty generous gift, then, I should say.'

Car? Brooke stared down at the keys in her palm and comprehension dawned. So did anger. 'Could you wait there a moment, please?'

Turning on her heel, she stalked down the corridor to the staffroom. Was Jed there? Maybe not. She hadn't seen him since he'd left the delivery room, but she knew from hearing snatches of conversation that there was another woman in difficulties so he wouldn't have gone far.

'Jed!' She crashed through the door, her eyes blazing, and he came to his feet in a fluid movement, concern in his blue eyes.

'What's happened?'

'How—how could you!'

He stared at her for a moment and then gave a smile of comprehension. 'Oh, right. They've delivered your new car.'

'How could you do that?' She put her hands on her hips and glared at him. 'How could you when you know I don't want your money?'

'I'm not giving you money, Brooke,' he said reasonably, settling himself back down in the chair, totally undaunted by her anger. 'I'm giving you a car. One that works and isn't likely to fall apart or cause a major accident. One that you can drive our son around in safely.'

'But I don't want a car.'

He lifted an eyebrow. 'You're happy taking two buses and travelling home at the dead of night?'

'Well, no.' She bit her lip. 'But—'

'So you were going to find another car.' His voice was annoyingly calm. 'But I've saved you the trouble.'

'I don't want you to save me the trouble.'

He sat back in his chair and laughed with genuine amusement. 'Are you a masochist? Why is it that you feel the need to make life as hard as possible?'

'I just don't want you to buy me a car! I don't want to owe you anything.'

He sighed. 'It's a gift. No strings attached.'

Suddenly he made her feel hideously ungrateful.

'Everything has strings attached.' Her voice was gruff and he smiled gently.

'No strings.'

She stared uncertainly at the keys in her hand and he stood up and walked over to where she was standing.

'It seems to me that so far in your life no one has ever given you a single thing without demanding payment or making you feel guilty. Until now.' He lifted her chin and his eyes were gentle. 'That's all this is, Brooke. Just a gift.'

Her heart thudded as she stared into his blue eyes and her fingers closed around the keys. She did need a car badly...

'OK, then, but it's not a gift,' she said fiercely. 'I'll pay you back.'

He shrugged. 'I don't need your money and there's nothing to pay. You don't owe me anything.'

She was adamant. 'I don't want money from you, Jed.'

'Well, that's a novelty,' he drawled, brushing her cheek with his knuckles. 'A woman who doesn't want a man's money. I've got to dash, I'm afraid. I've got an antenatal clinic, but I'll call round tomorrow and fix your roof.'

'Jed—'

'Don't even say it!' He rolled his eyes in exasperation.

'You don't want me to fix your roof! You want it to carry on leaking. You're a crazy woman, do you know that?'

'I don't need you to fix my roof!' She glared at him and he glared back, but his firm mouth twitched with humour.

'Well, tough! I'm fixing it or the whole thing will fall in.' He tugged open the door and turned, the humour suddenly fading from his handsome face. 'Oh, and, Brooke?'

She swallowed. 'What?'

His eyes challenged hers. 'I'd like to take Toby out tomorrow.'

Her heart twisted but she nodded slowly. What choice did she have?

None at all.

CHAPTER SIX

JED turned up first thing the next morning, looking refreshed and too handsome for his own good. 'I don't suppose there's any breakfast on offer?'

'You bought us a new car.' Toby looked at him with huge eyes. 'It doesn't make funny noises.'

Jed grinned. 'I'm jolly relieved to hear it.'

Toby was still looking at him and Jed crouched down, his eyes gentle.

'What's the matter, sport?'

'Cars cost a lot. Mum said.'

Jed shrugged. 'But you needed one.'

'Are you very rich?'

'Toby!' Brooke was aghast but Jed just laughed.

'Filthy rich, Toby. Why? Is there something you need?'

Brooke remembered Ally's comments and wondered just how rich he was. 'Jed, for goodness' sake—'

Jed lifted a hand to silence her, his eyes still on the boy. 'What did you want, old chap?'

Toby went bright red. 'I'm not supposed to ask for things...'

Jed's voice was gruff. 'Ask away, Toby.'

'David at school has got some puppies...'

Brooke groaned. 'Toby, no! We can't look after a dog, sweetheart. We're not at home enough. It isn't a matter of money. A dog needs company.'

Toby's face fell and Jed put a hand on his shoulder.

'Your mum's right. Owning a dog is a big responsibility. You have to be able to spend lots and lots of time with it and take it for walks. But I'll tell you what we'll do if you like animals...'

'What?' Toby's body still drooped miserably. 'I like dogs best and then horses, but I don't suppose I can have one of those either.'

'Well, it might be a bit cramped in your cottage if you shared it with a horse,' Jed teased, squeezing his shoulder gently. 'Cheer up. By the time you come home tonight you'll have spent so much time with dogs and horses you'll be worn out with them.'

'Why?' Toby's eyes widened. 'Where are we going?'

'It's a surprise. Go upstairs and change into old trousers, grab a warm coat and your wellies, and we'll leave in half an hour.'

'Leave for where?' Toby danced on the spot, the prospect of owning a dog forgotten.

'It's a secret.' Jed turned to Brooke. 'I was going to do the roof this morning, but on second thoughts we'll go out now and I'll sort the roof out later. If that's all right with you.'

'I've had the roof fixed,' she told him stiffly. 'Temporarily at least. They came just before you this morning.'

The truth was, she didn't care about the roof—it was Jed taking Toby that worried her. But what choice did she have? She licked dry lips and blushed as his gaze dropped to her mouth. She was so aware of him that every nerve in her body tingled.

'I can't stop you taking him, Jed, but I'd like to know where the two of you are going.'

'The two of us?' He frowned and looked at her quizzically. 'I wasn't planning to take him on my own. I thought you'd come, too.'

She stared at him. He wanted her, too? 'I assumed you'd want him to yourself.'

'You assume a lot of things that aren't true,' he said wryly, lifting a hand and stroking her dark hair away from her face. His fingers stroked her forehead and lingered on her cheek as his eyes searched hers. 'Did I ever tell you that you have fabulous hair?'

His rough, male voice was so sexy that she felt her limbs tremble.

'Jed, please...'

'Did I ever tell you that?' His voice was softly insistent and she nodded and looked away.

She couldn't bear to remember how he'd stroked her hair and how he'd wound it round his strong hands to hold her face still for his kiss.

'Where are we going?' She dragged herself away from him and made for the fridge. 'What do I need to wear? And what do you want to eat? Bacon sandwich or something healthier? Yoghurt, fruit?'

'Bacon sounds great and you're fine as you are. Jeans suit you.' His gaze slid over her gently rounded hips and long legs. 'You might need a warm jumper and boots. It can be muddy.'

Brooke laid the bacon under the grill and cut some bread. 'You're not going to tell me where we're going?'

'No.' He filled the kettle and glanced round the kitchen. 'It's a surprise. Where do you keep your mugs?'

'In that cupboard.' She gestured with her head, flipping the bacon over with a fork and trying to calm her pulse rate. Having him this close was very unnerving.

'I'm ready, Mum.' Toby jumped back into the room, wearing his wellingtons and clutching his coat.

She smiled. 'Well, sit down for two minutes while we have some breakfast.'

They sat round the table and munched bacon sandwiches while Toby chatted away, his excitement evident.

'Do I need to make a picnic?' Brooke looked at Jed, trying not to focus on his dark jawline and strong neck. He was just a man. Nothing special. She closed her eyes briefly. Who was she kidding? Jed Matthews was one in a million. It was just that he could never be hers. He might find her attractive, but it was no more than that.

'No. I've got plans for lunch.' His eyes narrowed as they fixed on her face. 'You've gone pale. Is something wrong?'

Everything.

'Nothing.' She summoned up a smile and piled the dishes in the washing-up bowl for later. 'Come on, then. Let's go.'

Jed drove for about forty minutes and then took a sharp right up a narrow track that led down a valley.

'Where are we going?' Toby had his nose pressed to the window, his breath clouding the window. 'I can see horses—and cows. Wow!'

'This is my parents' farm,' Jed told him, and Brooke swivelled in her seat, her eyes accusing.

'You're taking us to meet your parents?' She stared at him in disbelief. 'Without warning me?'

'Why not?' He tightened his grip on the steering wheel as they lurched into a pothole. 'I wish they'd sort out this lane.'

'No, Jed. No!' She raked her dark hair away from her face with a shaking hand. 'Who will you say we are?'

'What's the matter, Mummy?'

Brooke closed her eyes and sagged against the plush seat. She'd forgotten Toby was there.

'Nothing, darling.' She lowered her voice as she talked to Jed. 'We can't just suddenly turn up with no warning—'

'They've been warned,' Jed said quietly, his fingers gripping the wheel as he negotiated more ditches. 'It's just you I didn't warn, because I knew you'd react like this. Relax. You'll have a nice time. Trust me.'

Brooke nibbled her lip anxiously. 'Who do they think we are?'

Jed pulled up in front of a gorgeous rambling farmhouse and gave her a lopsided grin. 'Let's not worry about that now, hmm?'

He was out of the car before she could stop him, swinging Toby into his arms and making for the front door. She had no choice but to follow, her legs feeling like lead.

'How could you do this to me with no warning?' she hissed in his ear, and his eyes gleamed.

'Would you have come if I'd warned you?'

She bristled. 'Of course not!'

'Precisely why I didn't tell you,' he murmured, shifting Toby a bit higher as he grabbed the doorhandle and opened the front door. 'Anyone home?'

He strode into the hall and suddenly there was utter mayhem as four dogs surged towards them, barks and fur flying.

'Here we are, Toby. You wanted dogs.' Jed grinned and held him securely in his arms. 'My parents have four.'

Toby stared, wide-eyed, as the dogs panted and whined around the visitors, and then an attractive woman in her late fifties came down the stairs and gave them a warm welcome.

'Jed!' She reached up to hug her son and then gave Toby a special smile. 'And you must be Toby. I've heard about you.'

What had she heard? Brooke felt frighteningly vulnerable but Jed's mother gave her a warm hug and slipped an arm through hers, making it impossible for her to feel anything but welcome.

'Come and sit in the kitchen, dear. It's where everything happens in this house. Jed's father is out on a call but he shouldn't be long.'

Brooke remembered Jed saying that he was a vet. 'I hope we're not disturbing you, Mrs Matthews,' she said stiffly, but Jed's mother gave a shake of her head.

'Not at all, and, please, call me Ellie. We've one vet and two doctors in this family and that's quite enough of the medical profession, I can tell you. Our dinner-table conversation is quite hideous enough, believe me. Talking of which, Tom is here on a visit.'

'Really?' Jed lifted an eyebrow as he lowered Toby, still keeping hold of his hand. 'Great! Where is he?'

'In bed,' his mother replied dryly, lifting a whistling kettle off the Aga and filling up a teapot. 'You know your brother. He lives life in the fast lane.'

'Somebody has to,' came a sleepy drawl from behind them, and a more boyish version of Jed strolled into the room. 'Is that my big brother I hear?'

The two brothers greeted each other warmly, and before she knew what was happening Brooke found herself seated at the table, nursing a cup of tea, while cheerful banter swirled around the room.

She watched as Mrs Matthews plied them with food and joined in the conversation, fielding dogs and phone calls as she did so. This was the family life that she'd dreamed of when she'd been little. This was what she'd read about in books but never actually seen.

Watching the two brothers tease their mother unmercifully, she felt a lump in her throat. Having a loving family, that was the best thing that could happen to anyone. Better than anything else that life could give you.

She sneaked a look at Jed's mother, noticing the pride and love in her eyes as she laughed with her sons, noticing the caring way she welcomed Toby and produced food and drink as if it was a great pleasure. There was no sign of impatience. No suggestion that this woman would rather be doing anything but looking after her family.

Just watching them made Brooke feel like an outsider. She'd never been part of a family like this one, where everyone was loved and made to feel as though they were important. What would it be like to have someone actually caring what sort of day you'd had? What was it like to have someone tease you out of love and affection and to laugh with you? There had rarely been any laughter in her house.

Swallowing hard, she caught Jed's mother watching her keenly and looked away awkwardly. If she could just get through the next few hours she could fall apart in the privacy of her own home.

'Can I, Mum?'

She blinked and realised that Toby had been talking to her. 'Can you what, sweetheart?'

'Can I go and see the pony with Jed's mummy?'

Brooke smiled. 'Of course you can. But be careful.'

She stood up to help Toby put on his coat, her long dark hair trailing over her slim shoulders. Watching them go out into the yard, she was suddenly aware of Tom's curious gaze.

'Dammit, Jed.' He frowned at her and then glanced from her to his brother.

'Language, Tom,' his brother reproved mildly, but Tom ignored him, his eyes fixed on Brooke, who shifted uncomfortably. Why was he staring?

'Jed?' Tom was looking at his brother now and Jed sighed.

'Drop it, Tom.'

Brooke swallowed, brushing her hair away from her face self-consciously. Drop what? And then she remembered. Tom had known about that night. But surely he wouldn't know it was her?

'"Dark and delicate with legs like a gazelle",' Tom recited, and Jed gave him a look which made his younger brother subside. 'Sorry—still tired after last night. Don't know what I'm saying.'

Brooke stared at them both and suddenly had to get away. It was all too much, first being in the spotlight and then all the family togetherness. It just reminded her too much of what she'd never had and never would have. And on top of that Tom had clearly guessed who she was.

'I need some air.' She reached for her coat and gave them something approaching a smile. 'I'll be back later. Enjoy your chat.'

Without giving them time to respond, she tugged open the door and walked quickly across the yard in the opposite direction to her son. The path led her past two fields where cows grazed to a wide stream. Finding a flat rock, she sat down and hugged her knees, staring at the water as it flew past, twigs and leaves twirling in the current. That was how she felt, she thought miserably. She was just dragged along by the current of life, with no real security.

'I'm sorry about Tom.' Jed's deep voice made her jump but she didn't turn round. No way was she going to let him see her crying again.

'It doesn't matter.' She picked up a twig and tossed it into the stream, watching as it spun round and raced after the others.

'I told him about you all those years ago because he was my only hope of finding you. To be honest, I'm amazed he remembered. I'm sorry he was so tactless.' Jed squatted down next to her and turned her face towards him, cursing softly as he saw the tears. 'Sweetheart, I'm sorry. Please, don't cry.'

She shook her head. 'I'm not crying because of Tom.'

He frowned. 'What, then? Tell me, Brooke.'

She jerked her face away from him and stared back at the stream. 'It's nothing important. Really.'

'Jed?' The sound of his mother's voice came from quite close by and Jed growled in frustration.

'We're going to talk about this later. Come with me now. Toby wants to know if he can have a riding lesson with Mum.'

She stood up and met his eyes, her expression bleak. 'Does it really matter what I think, Jed? Won't you just do it anyway?'

'Is that why you're upset? Because you think I'm bullying you?' He stroked a strand of dark hair away from her face and his thumb grazed her cheek. 'I don't really have much choice. You fight me all the way on everything.'

She closed her eyes. It was just for her own protection, but he didn't know that, of course. If she wasn't fighting him she'd be asking him to love her, and she knew he couldn't do that.

'You're right.' She opened her eyes and gave him a tired smile. 'I'm being totally unreasonable. Of course Toby should ride. He'll love it.'

And he did love it.

Brooke stood on the bottom rung of the gate next to Jed, watching while Ellie led him around on a small grey Shetland pony.

'I learned to ride on that pony,' Jed told her, leaning his

arms on the gate and watching Toby. 'In fact, he taught us all to ride.'

'You're incredibly lucky,' Brooke said gruffly, her eyes fixed on her son as he held the saddle, his face glowing with excitement and happiness.

Jed turned to face her, his eyes searching. 'I know that, Brooke. Is that why you're upset? Seeing my family?'

She swallowed and turned her head away so that he couldn't see her face. 'When I was a little girl I used to have this fantasy.'

'Which was?'

She could tell from his voice that he was no longer looking at Toby and that his eyes were fixed on her instead.

'We lived in a beautiful farmhouse in the country and I had lots of brothers and sisters to play with and animals all around me. There were mountains and streams and we'd go for walks and usually I'd get into trouble.'

His voice was soft. 'What sort of trouble?'

'Oh, it varied.' She stared across the fields, feeling the weak March sun on her face. 'It didn't really matter, but I always needed to be rescued and my dad was always there for me, keeping me out of trouble because he loved me.'

Jed gave a soft curse and turned her to face him, brushing her dark hair away from her face with a gentle hand. 'That shouldn't have been a fantasy. That should have been a reality. Not the farmhouse and the countryside, but the love and protection of your father. That's what family life is about.'

She shook her head. 'Not for everyone, Jed.'

He gave a sigh and released her, leaning on the gate again and watching Toby. 'I do understand now why you didn't want to tell me about him. Why you don't want us to have a relationship.'

'Good.' She gave him a half smile. 'At least that should make things easier between us.'

'Easier?' He gave a short laugh and rubbed his forehead with long fingers. 'It makes it harder than ever.'

She stared at him 'Why harder?'

'Because I *do* want us to have a relationship, Brooke.' He turned to face her, the expression in his blue eyes determined as they locked with hers. 'And, believe me, we are going to have one. But I'm prepared to be patient and wait until you also realise that it's the right thing.'

She shook her head, her breathing unsteady. 'Jed, I've told you—'

'And I heard you.' His eyes narrowed slightly, thick dark lashes shielding his expression from her. 'But you can stop telling me, Brooke, because I'm not listening any more. We had a relationship before Toby came along, remember?'

Remember? She remembered every minute detail. 'Just one night, Jed.'

'So?' He shrugged, totally unconcerned, and turned back to watch Toby. 'Every relationship has to start somewhere— it's just that our beginning was somewhat...explosive. What we need to do now is get to know each other and take it gently.'

'Gently?'

'Yes.' He gave her a sexy grin. 'By that I mean that we don't touch each other. We both know that when we touch each other we can't think straight. So no touching. For now at least.'

She stared at him. 'You're more stubborn than I am!'

'You'd better believe it, Brooke.' His jaw was set and determined as he watched Toby circle the field. 'He's good. Relaxed, and he sits well. He ought to have lessons. I'll talk to Mum.'

'Jed!' Brooke glared at him. 'You can't just arrange for him to have lessons with your mum. Your mum may not want him around.'

'He's her grandchild.' Jed's gaze was still fixed on Toby but his voice was firm. 'Of course she wants him around.'

'Does she know, Jed?' Brooke's voice was hoarse and she tugged at his arm, feeling the solid muscle under her fingers. 'Are you saying you've told her?'

Jed nodded. 'Yes, actually. My parents are very liberal. We don't go in for secrets, I'm afraid.'

'How could you do that?' Brooke groaned and dropped her head into her hands. 'Oh, dear God, what must she think of me?'

'You? I don't think she thinks anything bad of you. A person only has to look at you to see you're as innocent as the day you were born. It's me that's in trouble,' Jed pointed out, removing her hands from her face and laughing into her eyes. 'She thinks I'm a big bad boy and that I led you astray. Which is the truth, as we both know.'

Brooke bit her lip. 'But she must hate me for not having told you—'

'She doesn't hate you. She respects your reasons.' Jed gave a wry smile. 'Probably more than her son does.'

'But what now?' Brooke stared at him in horror and shook her head. 'Is she expecting us to get together?'

She felt the panic bubble up inside her. She didn't want Jed to have more pressure—

'Calm down.' His fingers closed over her shoulders and his blue eyes were infinitely gentle. 'You worry too much, do you know that? You spend your whole life worrying and analysing things. Forget it, Brooke. Just relax and get to know me and my family. There's no pressure, sweetheart. None at all.'

His gentle endearment made her insides melt and she wished that she could have met this man under different circumstances. Maybe then—

'Mum, Mum, did you see me?' Toby came racing towards her, Jed's mother leading the pony behind him.

They unsaddled the pony and took him back to the field and then walked back to the farmhouse for lunch.

'Could you heat the soup for me, dear?' Ellie handed Brooke a bowl of home-made soup from the fridge and soon she was involved in preparing lunch with everyone else, with no time to feel self-conscious or out of place.

Tom was on good form, making everyone laugh with his

stories of London life, and halfway through lunch Jed's father arrived, trailing mud into the kitchen.

Jed's mother rolled her eyes as she placed a huge bowl of soup in front of him. 'Did you leave any mud at all at the Baxters' farm or is it all on your boots?'

'There's none on his boots,' Tom pointed out wickedly. 'It's all on the kitchen floor.'

His father glared at him. 'Thank you, Tom, for that contribution to marital harmony.'

Brooke smiled, knowing that there was plenty of marital harmony in this house. Their warmth and happiness was so contagious it sucked you in and made you a part of it. Suddenly she didn't feel like an outsider any more, and when she caught Jed watching her she managed a shy smile.

Jed's father was charming and it was easy to see where Jed got his incredible looks from. Even in his late fifties, Peter Matthews was a handsome man.

'So...I don't suppose any of you strapping lads could help me clear out the shed this afternoon?'

Tom rubbed his shoulder and winced. 'I've got this rugby injury...'

'You'll have more than a rugby injury if you don't give your father some help,' his mother said tartly, taking away his soup plate and giving him a nudge. 'Get up, you lazy hound. Brooke and I did the first course, it's your turn. There's cheese and ham in the fridge, and you and Jed can make a dressing for the salad.'

Tom looked at Jed, his eyes gleaming. 'Can we?'

Jed's eyes danced and he assumed a worried expression. 'Don't know really...'

Ellie put her hands on her hips and Jed stood up and grinned at her.

'OK, don't get in a state. It's not good for you at your age.'

'My age?'

And so it went on until Brooke felt as though she'd never had a happier day in her life. And Toby was enjoying himself, too, petting the dogs until Brooke was afraid they might be fed up with the attention.

By the time they'd said their goodbyes and piled into Jed's car, it was ten o'clock and Toby had been asleep for hours on the Matthews' comfortable sofa.

'Your family are wonderful,' Brooke said softly as they lifted the sleeping boy into the car and drove back down the lane, Jed cursing fluently under his breath as his car lurched into potholes.

'Did you have a nice time?'

She nodded. 'You know I did.'

'You seemed happy.'

She smiled in the darkness. 'I was.'

And it was true. At some point during the day she'd stopped feeling like an outsider and started feeling as though she were a part of that wonderful family, and it had felt so good.

'Your mum is lovely.'

Jed nodded. 'She missed us so much when we were all in London. Now she's got two of her boys living in the same county she's a happy woman. She loves nothing better than having hordes of people around her kitchen table.'

'Does she ever—' Brooke broke off as the car in front of them braked suddenly, skidding across the road and exploding through a low stone wall before coming to a halt in a field. 'Oh, my God! Jed!'

'Stay with Toby! And call an ambulance!' Jed ordered, jerking on his handbrake and leaving the car at a run.

Brooke fumbled in his coat pocket for his mobile phone and called for an ambulance, before checking that Toby was still asleep. Anxiously she glanced at Jed and realised that he probably couldn't see a thing because of the darkness. Praying that he wasn't too territorial about his precious car, she slid across into the driver's seat and started the engine, driving it a few yards along the road to the safety of a gateway and putting the headlights on full beam.

'At least now he should be able to see what he's doing,'

she muttered, checking Toby again before leaving the car and sprinting towards the accident.

Jed was still trying to open the passenger door, his foot planted on the car as he tried to get more leverage.

'Someone help us!' The man in the driver's seat was obviously conscious and in pain, and Jed redoubled his efforts.

'We're doing our best. The door must have buckled on impact.' He braced himself and then yanked at the door with all his strength. It groaned and opened reluctantly with a sickening sound of tearing metal. Jed glanced over his shoulder and glowered at Brooke. 'You shouldn't be here! It isn't safe to leave Toby in the car.'

'I've moved the car off the road,' she told him briskly, 'and I've locked it. He'll be fine and you need help.'

'Get my wife out.' The man was sobbing now, panic evident in his face. 'Get my wife out.'

'We'll get both of you out, sir,' Jed said calmly, feeling the woman's pulse and frowning at Brooke.

'What's the matter?' She was by his side in an instant and he lowered his voice so that the woman's husband couldn't hear.

'There's a hell of a lot of blood here and I don't know where it's coming from. Damn, the light's non-existent!'

'She's pregnant.' The driver spoke again, his voice little more than a groan. 'My wife's pregnant.'

'How pregnant?' Jed asked urgently, loosening the woman's seat belt and glancing up as the shriek of an ambulance siren cut through the night air. 'How pregnant is your wife?'

'I can't remember—about twenty-five weeks, I think. Yes, twenty-five weeks.'

The woman groaned and Jed crouched down beside her, his voice calm. 'You're all right, I'm a doctor. What's your name?'

'Linda.' The woman winced and stifled a sob. 'The pain's terrible.'

'OK, we'll do something about that straight away,' Jed

assured her, glancing up as the paramedics sprinted across to them, carrying powerful torches.

'What have we got?'

'Male who I haven't assessed yet,' Jed told them grimly, 'but he's talking. His wife is pregnant. I need to see to her—can I leave the man to one of you?'

The paramedic who stayed to assist with Linda narrowed his eyes at Jed and then grinned. 'It's Mr Matthews, isn't it? Great. An obstetrician on site is a pretty lucky break.'

'For whom?' Jed replied dryly, working with him to stabilise the woman's spine before lifting her from the car onto the stretcher. 'At least your lights have improved the visibility. Now, Linda, I need to take a look at you. Are you sure you're twenty-five weeks?'

The woman nodded and Jed tugged on some gloves provided by the paramedics and examined her, feeling the height of the uterus with a frown.

Brooke lifted her eyes to his. 'Retroplacental bleed,' she mouthed, and he nodded briefly.

'Looks that way.' He turned back to the woman, his voice calm and steady. 'Linda, your uterus is bigger than it should be and I suspect you might be bleeding behind your placenta. We need to get you to hospital.'

'It was a fox.'

'Sorry?' Brooke blinked and knelt down next to the woman. 'What was a fox?'

'Martin swerved to avoid a fox.' She was sobbing quietly now and Brooke soothed her gently, holding her hand while Jed helped her into the right position.

'She needs to get to hospital fast.' Jed lifted his head and said to the paramedic, 'Daniel, could you get some equipment here, please?'

'What do you need, Mr Matthews?'

'I need two 16 gauge cannulas. I want to give her one hundred per cent oxygen and I want to give her intravenous colloid.'

'Coming right up.' Daniel sprinted to the ambulance and returned with armfuls of equipment. 'Two cannulas...'

'Right. Squeeze her arm for me, Brooke.' Jed gritted his teeth and breathed a sigh of relief as the first cannula slid home. 'Now the other one.'

Soon that was in too, and Jed had attached an infusion set while Brooke attached the oxygen.

'OK, guys, let's get her straight to the infirmary,' he instructed, straightening and glancing across to the husband as the second paramedic came over to assist. 'How's he doing?'

'He's fine, actually. Nasty cut on his scalp and he may have broken a couple of ribs, but he's a lucky guy. Could have been a lot worse for him.'

Jed glanced at Brooke and she knew what he was thinking. If they didn't get to hospital soon, things would be a lot worse. Linda was in a very bad way.

CHAPTER SEVEN

BROOKE followed the ambulance in Jed's car, amazed that Toby was still asleep. When they arrived at the infirmary they rushed Linda straight up to theatre so that Jed could examine her properly. Brooke knew that he was worried that the placenta could be positioned low in the uterus, and any internal examination could trigger a severe haemorrhage. If he had her safely in theatre then at least he would be able to deal with the possible consequences of the examination.

Scooping her sleeping son out of the car, Brooke carried him up to the labour ward, laid him on the couch in the staffroom and covered him with a blanket.

'I hear you've had a drama.' Gill, who was still there long after she should have been off duty, popped her head round the door and gave her a curious look. 'Jed's gone into theatre now—do you need anything?'

Brooke shook her head, suddenly realising that the entire unit would now know that she'd arrived with Jed. Oh, well...

She made herself comfortable and settled down with a magazine and a coffee to wait for news, but it was an hour before Jed opened the door and strode into the room, his face strained.

'What happened?' She scrambled to her feet and he shook his head, his expression grim.

'She had a massive haemorrhage. We stopped it eventually and the baby's alive, but only just. It's a tiny thing.' He rubbed the bridge of his nose with his fingers and gave her a sad smile. 'They're devastated, of course, but the truth is that Linda's lucky to be alive at all. She lost a hell of a lot of blood.'

'If you hadn't been there she probably wouldn't have made it,' Brooke said quietly, handing him a coffee. He looked so exhausted and depressed that she wanted to hug him, but she didn't dare. They didn't have that sort of relationship. 'Has the baby gone to Special Care?'

Jed nodded and sipped his coffee. 'They're sorting the little scrap out now, but it isn't looking good. Oh, well. Is Toby still asleep?'

'Certainly is.' Brooke smiled at her son. 'All that fresh air, I suppose. If you don't mind giving us a lift home, I'll put him straight to bed.'

'Of course. I'm not on call tonight anyway.' Jed drained his cup and scooped Toby into his arms.

Brooke was horribly aware of Gill's speculative gaze as they left the unit, but she forced herself to ignore it. She'd deal with the inevitable questions tomorrow.

In the weeks that followed it seemed to Brooke that she and Jed were thrown together constantly, and whatever her misgivings about their personal relationship she had none about their professional one. They understood each other well and Brooke was amazed that Jed was so in tune with her own thinking about labour and delivery.

He tried never to intervene unless he had to, and actively encouraged a more 'natural' approach as long as there was no risk involved to mother or baby. He also clearly respected Brooke's opinion, which she found refreshingly touching. She'd worked with plenty of obstetricians who showed little respect for midwives, and Jed's skill at fostering true team spirit did much to raise morale on the unit.

He was warm and patient with the mums but his real skill was in judging just when to intervene. He seemed to have an intuitive feel for trouble and his skill and confidence in the operating theatre had averted several potentially dangerous situations.

'You're always so cool and confident. Don't you ever feel self-doubt?' she asked him curiously after he'd finished a particularly tricky emergency section, which Gill had predicted would have an unhappy ending. Thanks to Jed it hadn't, and both mother and baby were alive and expected to do well.

He raised a dark eyebrow. 'You want to be operated on by a surgeon who doubts himself? You want me to start every operation by saying, "Mrs Brown, you may be nervous, but you're not half as nervous as I am''?' His eyes gleamed with humour. 'I can't quite see it filling her with confidence, can you?'

Brooke laughed, too. 'You know I didn't mean it that way!' She blushed slightly. 'It's just—well, you're always so self-assured. I wondered if it was really an act.'

Those blue eyes welded to hers and he dragged his fingertips down his cheeks in a gesture of affection. 'Well, I never had the stuffing knocked out of me when I was young.' His voice was gruff. 'My self-confidence has always been carefully nurtured thanks to my privileged family life.'

But Brooke knew there was more to it than that. Jed was a strong person, outside and inside, and his self-confidence was part of that strength.

At least once a week Jed took her over to the farm and Ellie gave Toby a riding lesson while Jed and Brooke watched or walked together through the fields. Tom had gone back to London but occasionally Phil, Jed's older brother, was there, usually discussing some crisis about one of the properties.

Always Brooke was made to feel welcome and, seated at the huge kitchen table covered in magazines, riding equipment and the results of Ellie's baking, she felt totally at home, surrounded by warmth and safer than she'd felt in her life.

Toby's parentage wasn't mentioned until one weekend when they arrived to find the whole family, including Tom and Phil, gathered round the kitchen table which was loaded with presents and a huge birthday cake.

'Happy Birthday!' they chorused as she and Toby walked

through the door, and Brooke stared at them, stunned. She couldn't remember the last time anyone had celebrated her birthday with her except Toby.

'How did you know?' Her cheeks were pink and she looked at Jed who was grinning from ear to ear, visibly pleased with himself.

'Gill told me.'

Brooke felt a lump building in her throat. 'I don't know what to say...'

'Just blow out the candles,' Phil said dryly. 'We're all starving and this is the only cake in the house.'

After that typical Phil remark she couldn't help but laugh, shrugging off her jacket as she moved towards the table.

'Can I help?' Toby was dancing round next to her and she hugged him close.

'Of course. Ready?' They counted to three and blew, beaming as everyone cheered.

After that they all handed her their presents and she felt the lump in her throat return. 'You shouldn't have got me presents—'

'Of course we should.' Ellie walked across and gave her a hug. 'You're one of the family and everyone has presents on their birthday.'

One of the family. How she wished she was. But it wasn't true. Not really.

Blinking back tears, she tore open the first present and removed a beautiful silk top with matching trousers.

'Oh, they're stunning!' She gasped and smiled shyly at Jed's parents. 'Thank you so much.'

Toby proudly gave her a photograph frame that he'd been secretly making and painting with Ellie.

'It's beautiful, we'll have to choose a photo together.' She kissed him gently and he slipped onto her knee and sat happily while she opened the rest of her presents. Phil and Tom had given her soft leather gloves and Jed a gold bangle which she loved and immediately slipped onto her slim wrist.

Hideously self-conscious, she thanked them all again and was relieved when the conversation turned to the business again, which it invariably did when the whole Matthews family were together.

Later they wandered outside to check on some lambs that Ellie was hand-rearing and Brooke found herself alone with Jed's mother.

'Thank you for today,' Brooke said shyly, leaning into the shed to look at the lambs. 'The cake was delicious. A real treat.'

'You're very welcome,' Ellie said quietly, slipping an arm through hers, her eyes warm. 'I hope you consider yourself part of our family, Brooke.'

'You've only known me for a few weeks,' Brooke began, but Ellie shook her head with a smile.

'Time doesn't matter dear, it's how you feel about someone that matters. You belong here. The whole family loves you.'

Brooke looked up, startled. Was she referring to her relationship with Jed? 'Ellie—'

'Can I ask you something?' The older woman met her eyes frankly and Brooke bit her lip, wondering what was coming.

'Of course.'

'Do you love my son?'

Brooke stared at the lambs, feeling her colour rise. 'Yes.'

'I thought so.' Ellie nodded calmly. 'Thank you for being honest. So it's not a lack of feeling that's the problem, but a lack of trust. You don't trust him, and I can hardly blame you for that, given your miserable experience of family life. Jed told me, by the way—I hope you don't mind.'

Brooke shook her head and closed her eyes briefly. 'I must have shocked you terribly…'

'For falling for Jed like a stone? Hardly!' Jed's mother gave a snort. 'I was the same about his father, let me tell you.'

'Really?' Brooke looked at her curiously. 'Did you fall in love with him in one night?'

'In one hour, actually.' Ellie stared dreamily at the lambs, her mind far away. 'I'd never been so bowled over by anybody. It was as if my mind and body were no longer under my control.'

'That's how I felt,' Brooke said, and then groaned. 'But, please, please, don't tell him.'

Ellie sighed. 'No, of course I won't tell him if you don't want me to, but if it's any consolation I'm sure he loves you, too.'

Brooke swallowed. 'Has he said so?'

'No.' Ellie was honest. 'He would never discuss that sort of thing with me. But I do know that women have been chasing Jed since infant school and I've never seen him look at anyone the way he looks at you.'

'That's just because of Toby,' Brooke said hoarsely, but Ellie shook her head.

'I really don't think so.' She reached out and covered Brooke's hand with her own. 'I'm not interfering, dear. We may be a very close family but we each like our own space, Jed especially. It's just that I'm very aware that you don't have your own mother to lean on, and I want you to try and forget that I'm Jed's mum. If you need a shoulder, then mine's here, waiting for you.'

With a sniff Brooke gave the older woman a hug, her cheeks damp as she felt loved and accepted for the first time in her whole life.

The rest of the afternoon passed quickly and, despite the earlier sunshine, it was raining heavily by the time Jed gave them a lift back to the cottage.

Brooke opened the door and stopped dead with a gasp of horror. 'Oh, no, Jed!'

'What's the matter?'

Jed was right behind her with Toby, and he moved them to one side, looking down as he felt what she'd felt. The hall carpet was squishy with water. He glanced up at the huge damp circle in the ceiling and then took the stairs two at a time to Toby's old bedroom. It wasn't long before he came back down.

'Part of the roof has come down and it's brought the ceiling with it,' he said flatly. 'The water must have come through to the hall.'

Brooke shook her head in disbelief. 'I don't believe it. They said they'd mended it...'

Jed made an instant decision and stopped her going for the phone. 'Leave it now, Brooke. We can't do anything tonight anyway. Pack some essentials for you two and we'll sort it out tomorrow. I'll sit in the car with Toby.'

He and Toby went out of the front door and back to the car, leaving Brooke to go up to her room and bundle a few things into a suitcase, her brain numb with shock. What was she going to do now?

She lugged the suitcase downstairs and Jed left the shelter of the car to stow it in the boot.

'I ought to try and do something about the roof but, frankly, I don't know who to call. Obviously the company I chose were a load of cowboys.' She blinked as the rain stuck to her lashes and Jed gave her a gentle push towards the car.

'Get in. I've already sorted it out.' He slid in next to her, his dark hair glistening with raindrops. 'You'll probably kill me for it but I just rang a friend of mine who's a roofer. He's going to come and take a look and use a tarpaulin or something.'

'Thanks.' Brooke subsided against the comfortable seat and Jed threw her a surprised look.

'Aren't you going to say, "How dare you interfere, Jed?"'

Brooke closed her eyes and gave a weak smile. 'I tried doing it myself and failed. I know when I'm beaten.'

Jed reached across and squeezed her hand, his voice gruff. 'You're not beaten, sweetheart, and, believe me, I'll be in contact with the people who did your roof.' His voice held a quiet menace that made her glance at him in surprise. Never in her whole life had anyone fought battles for her and, if she was honest, it felt good. She almost felt sorry for the roofer. Jed could be a formidable adversary when crossed as she already knew at first hand.

Determined not to be a pathetic female, Brooke rallied her flagging spirits and glanced over to the back seat to check on Toby who'd fallen asleep, exhausted by yet another exciting day.

'Where are we going, anyway?' She hadn't even asked that one, simple question.

'My house.' Jed reversed the car and turned back onto the main road, his car a haven of warmth and comfort against the lashing rain.

'Your house?' Brooke licked dry lips and stared at his very male profile. 'We can't stay with you—'

'You have a better suggestion?'

She didn't, but somehow it didn't seem right and her heart raced. 'Jed, we can't—'

'You'll be quite safe.' His tone was gently mocking. 'I've got a "no touch" policy where you're concerned, remember?'

Brooke bit her lip. He made it sound so easy. The trouble was, not touching Jed was starting to drive her mad.

'We can't stay with you. It isn't right,' she fretted, the reality of the situation suddenly hitting home. 'I need to sort things out at home.'

'And that's easier done from somewhere dry and warm. Try and forget it now. We'll contact your insurance company in the morning.' He swung up a long drive and her eyes widened as she saw the beautiful house, partly hidden by trees. It was built entirely out of wood, with interesting angles and lots of glass with views onto the surrounding woodland and fells.

'You live here?' She looked at it in amazement and then at him. 'This is yours?'

He lifted an eyebrow and, unusually for Jed, looked suddenly unsure. 'You hate it?'

'Hate it?' Her eyes swivelled back to the house which blended so beautifully into the landscape. 'It's stunning. Like a sort of up-market log cabin.'

'Well, come and see inside.' He switched off the engine and lifted Toby carefully.

She followed him inside, her eyes feasting on the high ceilings, the huge expanse of glass and the warmth of his furnishings.

'I'll show you the bedrooms,' he murmured, taking her upstairs and shouldering open a door. 'You can sleep next door and then if he wakes he shouldn't have too much of a shock.'

He carefully undressed the boy and tucked him under the covers, before switching a lamp on next to the bed.

Then he pulled the door slightly and they went back downstairs to the kitchen.

'Glass of wine or gin and tonic?'

'Wine would be great.' She followed him, glancing around her in admiration. 'It's fabulous, Jed. Did you do it yourself?'

'Well, I didn't build it, if that's what you mean.' His eyes gleamed as he walked towards the fridge. 'But I did all electrics, heating and the interior. Because of the family business we're all pretty handy at DIY and we know all the local tradesmen.'

'It's incredible...' She wandered round his huge living room, staring at the squashy inviting sofas and the stunning prints on the walls. Despite her anxieties, she gave a chuckle and he looked up as he closed the fridge door, a bottle of white wine in his hand.

'What's funny?'

'The thought of Toby on your white sofas.' She giggled, her dark eyes dancing. 'I think you might change your mind about having us as house guests once he wakes up.'

Jed grinned in appreciation and yanked the cork out of

the bottle. 'Well, I might ban muddy wellies but apart from that I'll take my chances.'

'You're a brave man, then,' Brooke said dryly, taking a glass of wine with a smile of thanks. 'Toby is a real little boy, I'm afraid, without much respect for cleanliness, but you should know that by now, having seen him in action at your parents' house.'

'It's not a showpiece, Brooke,' he protested mildly, sinking into one of the sofas and stretching his long legs out in front of him. 'The house is meant to be lived in.'

She tried not to look at the firm muscle of his strong thighs or the breadth of his shoulders. He had an incredible physique. If she hadn't known how gentle he could be, his size would have been quite intimidating.

'Are you hungry?' He was watching her closely and she shook her head, hoping he couldn't read her thoughts. Having him so close was torture. She was desperate to touch him. Desperate. But she couldn't...

'I'm still full from lunch.' Her voice was husky and she gave him a slightly shy smile. 'Your mum's birthday cake is the best and she serves giant portions.'

He laughed. 'Well, that's true enough. She's used to feeding hungry men. You must want something to eat—I've got some nice cheese and some French bread. Does that appeal?'

'Delicious. I'll do it.' Brooke sprang up and walked towards the kitchen, anxious to put some distance between them. The temptation to touch him was so strong she was afraid she might do something stupid.

'You're very jumpy.' He stood up and followed her, his eyes searching. 'Is something wrong?'

She rummaged in the fridge, hiding her face. 'Nothing. I'm fine. Brie and Dolcelatte?'

'Sounds good.' He cut some French bread and tossed it into a basket, adding butter and fruit to a tray. 'Let's eat in front of the fire. It's such a foul night I need the comfort, and I bet you do, too.'

For the first time she realised that he'd lit the fire and it was now blazing merrily, the focal point for the huge living room.

He pulled up a table and moved one of the sofas closer, giving Brooke no choice but to sit down next to him. She sat as near the edge of the sofa as she could, and if he noticed, he didn't comment.

'So, talk to me, Brooke.' He handed her a plate filled with different bits and pieces and did the same for himself.

She put the plate on her knee and stared at him. 'Talk to you?'

'Yes. Over the past weeks we've talked about lots of things, but never details.' His firm mouth twitched slightly and he handed her a knife. 'I want details.'

'What sort of details?'

'Well, let's start with Toby.' He ate some grapes and spread some soft cheese onto his bread. 'What was he like as a baby? Did he go to playgroup? What was he interested in? Animals? Tractors?'

Brooke smiled. 'Well, both of those.' Haltingly at first she started to talk, filling him in on Toby's life from birth until his first day at school, painting a vivid picture of life with a lively little boy.

Jed listened carefully, occasionally refilling her wineglass or asking the odd question, but otherwise silent and attentive.

'And what about your delivery? What was that like?'

'Jed, for goodness' sake!' Brooke flushed with embarrassment and Jed laughed softly.

'I can't believe you're shy. We made him together, Brooke! Surely it's not that much of a personal question?'

It seemed very personal and she blushed even deeper as she filled him in on the details of her labour, which had fortunately been relatively trouble-free, despite Toby's prematurity.

'Did you feed him yourself?'

'Yes, although obviously he was tube-fed for the first few

weeks in Special Care. I expressed milk at first and then once he learned to suck I fed him myself.'

'Good for you.' Jed's eyes were warm. 'Lots of women with babies in Special Care have a problem getting them to breast-feed.'

'Well I must admit it wasn't easy,' Brooke said, her eyes softened by memories. 'Anyway, I carried on feeding him myself for a year, although it took quite a bit of effort to express milk while I was working. Employers aren't that enlightened about breast-feeding mothers.'

Jed was silent for a moment as he prodded a piece of cheese with his knife. 'And what about men?' His voice was gruff. 'Did you have relationships?'

There was a long silence and her heart thudded in her chest. The truth was that she'd loved Jed too much to even contemplate a relationship with another man, but there was no way she wanted him knowing that.

'A few,' she said vaguely, careful not to look at him. He'd already told her that she was a hopeless liar so she'd better change the subject quickly.

When he spoke his voice sounded oddly strained. 'So having Toby didn't ruin your love life, then?'

'Toby didn't ruin anything,' she said honestly. 'He was the best thing that ever happened to me and I wouldn't change anything.'

There was a long silence as he stared at her. 'Wouldn't you, Brooke? I would.' He lifted her chin with strong fingers and held her eyes with his. 'If I could change one thing it would have been to have woken up before you sneaked away from me. I never would have let you go, Brooke.'

She swallowed. 'And what good would that have done?'

'Well, for a start I would have known that you were pregnant and I could have helped you.'

She shook her head. 'And I would have refused your help.'

'You wouldn't have been given a choice,' he growled,

his eyes shooting flames, and her heart flipped over in her chest.

What would have happened if he *had* woken up? Would things have been different? Jed was a persistent man, there was no doubt about that. She'd known he was strong from the first moment they'd met, but not quite *how* strong. He certainly wouldn't have let her go without a fight. So, what if they *had* pursued the incredible chemistry that had drawn them together? What if they *had* started a relationship before she'd found out she was pregnant? Her brief fantasy of a life with Jed was rudely interrupted by a vision of her father and she shook herself. Dreaming was pointless.

'I would have just disappeared again.' She gave him a wan smile. 'Believe me, Jed, I'm just as stubborn as you.'

'No, really?' He teased her with gentle sarcasm, one long finger trailing down the curve of her cheek as he studied her face. 'That's probably why we strike sparks off each other.'

His deep voice teased her senses and ruffled every nerve ending in her body. She could feel the tension in him and knew he was fighting a wild urge to kiss her. And she wanted him to. Dear God, she wanted him to so badly, and yet what good would that do? Just provide more torture and more torment by reminding her of what she couldn't have.

'You said no touching, Jed.' Her voice was barely audible and she heard him draw a jerky breath, his blue eyes clouded with indecision.

'No touching—right.' He closed his eyes briefly and then released her, raking long fingers through his hair and giving her a wry smile. 'One of my more stupid ideas. OK, well, in that case you'd better talk a bit more. How on earth did you manage to carry on with your training?'

'I was extremely lucky.' Brooke watched as he strode across the room and took a slug of wine, his whole body rigid with tension. 'I found a childminder who was like a mother to both of us, and in the end we moved in and lodged with her.'

'And that was when you left home? After he was born?'

Brooke settled herself back down on the sofa and slipped off her shoes, curling her legs under her bottom. 'I left home before that.'

'Why?'

'My father didn't want me around once he knew I was pregnant. He was horrified by what the neighbours would think.'

The expression in his blue eyes was murderous. 'If I ever meet your father...'

'You won't. We're not in touch any more.' She managed a smile, touched by his protectiveness. 'And, anyway, it was a long time ago and I managed.'

'How, I will never know,' Jed said roughly, putting down his glass and staring into the fire. 'It's probably just as well I wasn't around. If I had been I'd have killed your father. You're an amazing woman, Brooke.'

'Why?' She gave him a surprised look. 'Leaving home was hardly a hardship, if I'm honest. I was very happy with Molly—that was the childminder.'

'So why did you leave London?'

'Well, unfortunately Molly's elderly mother needed looking after and she moved down to Devon to be with her.' Brooke picked at a piece of cheese. 'London was right out of my price range really and I hate cities, so I moved here.'

'Part of your fantasy...' Jed murmured, his blue eyes fixed on her face. 'Mountains and countryside.'

'That's right.' She kept her tone light but he paced over to her and crouched down in front of her, the look in his eyes doing peculiar things to her insides.

For a wild moment the desire to lean on those broad shoulders was almost overwhelming, but then she remembered her father. He was always there, sitting squarely in her subconscious, reminding her that Jed hadn't planned to have this child. That he hadn't chosen the responsibility of parenthood. That he didn't need her to lean on him.

'You were the one who asked me to tell you about my past. I wasn't angling for sympathy. I'm fine.'

He gave her a sexy, lopsided smile. 'Well, I'm glad one of us is. I'm dying of an advanced case of sexual frustration.'

'Don't!' With a slight sob she uncurled her legs and pushed him away, scooping up the plates and cheese and heading for the sanctuary of the kitchen. It didn't work. He was right behind her.

Brooke piled the plates into the sink until Jed calmly pointed out the dishwasher. She gritted her teeth, totally flustered. Of course, he would have a dishwasher. She bit her lip and loaded it, hoping she was putting things in the right place, painfully aware of him lounging in the doorway, scrutinising her every movement. The rain pounded a hypnotic rhythm on the roof, making the cosy interior of his house seem even more intimate, and suddenly she felt hideously shy of him.

'Brooke?' His voice was low and seductive and she turned to find herself only inches away from his powerful frame. For a moment she was paralysed, unable to do anything except lose herself in the depth of those blue eyes, and then she gave a murmur of protest and pushed past him.

'No, Jed. Don't look at me like that.'

She backed away and his eyes softened with humour.

'Like what?'

'I don't know,' she was breathless and confused by her feelings. Why did being close to this man always do this to her? 'Like you want to kiss me.'

'I want to do a lot more than that, as you well know.' Jed's voice was so close it affected her breathing. 'Brooke, look at me. Dammit, why are we torturing ourselves?'

He caught her firmly and turned her into his arms, his mouth finding hers in one determined, possessive movement. And she was lost.

This was no sensitive, exploratory kiss. No tentative seeking of pleasure. Instead his mouth plundered hers relentlessly, stirring her into a response of equal desperation. They were both starved of the other's touch, desperate to feed their burning need, and Brooke curled her hands into the hard muscle of his shoulders, drawing herself closer to his powerful body.

With a rough sound he captured her face in his hands, holding her still as his kiss deepened, the excitement threatening to overwhelm both of them. Brooke fumbled with his shirt, wondering which one of them was shaking more as she jerked it free of his trousers, leaving his warm, male flesh tantalising accessible. Her small hands slipped inside and she felt his reaction as she slid her soft palm gently over the heated flesh of his back. At last. To touch him again like this after so long felt so good. Too good.

Still their mouths clung, refusing to break the contact even as his hands tore at her clothing. When his hand cupped the fullness of her breast through her silky bra she gasped against his mouth and pressed closer, desperate to feel more of him, still more.

'Have you any idea how much I want you?' His hoarse words were barely comprehensible as he lifted her in one easy movement and set her down on the table, his mouth still ravishing hers as he wrapped her legs around his hard thighs, neither one of them able to halt the reaction that had exploded between them.

Her hands lifted to his face and she explored the roughness of his jaw and the contrasting softness of his dark hair. With a muttered oath he pulled her hard against him, their bodies straining towards each other until the desperation was almost a physical pain.

Brooke couldn't focus on anything except her overwhelming need for this man. The wild, uncontrollable expression of passion that exploded whenever they touched. In a breathless confusion of excitement she felt him, hard and thoroughly male, through the soft material of his trousers and she knew that she wanted him with every fibre of her being.

'Brooke...' Her name was a groan on his lips as he stoked the heat between them, fuelling their desperation until they were both fevered and panting. 'The bed, sweetheart.' He muttered the words against her skin as he pressed open-mouthed kisses down the creamy skin of her throat. 'This time we're going to make it to bed.'

Bed? Suddenly the clouds in her head cleared and she pushed against his broad shoulders, her breath coming in rapid pants. Bed? Dear God, what was she doing? She'd never meant this to happen.

'No, Jed.' She tried to wriggle herself free but she was trapped by his powerful body, her own slim legs wrapped around his hard thighs. 'We can't do this.'

'We can.' His voice was a low growl and his dark head bent towards hers, but she shied away, knowing that if she let him kiss her again she'd be lost. It was always that way with Jed. He could make her his with one touch of his mouth.

'No, Jed.' She pushed him frantically, her dark hair falling in a tangle around her shoulders. 'This is torture. It's worse than torture.'

His breathing was laboured and his eyes were still burning with what had flared between them. 'It doesn't have to be torture, Brooke.'

She shook her head, fighting her own impulses with a desperate effort and lashings of will power. 'No. We can't do this. Not like this. Not again.'

He held her for a long moment, his body still pressed intimately against hers, and then he released her suddenly, his breathing harsh and uneven. 'You're right, of course, this isn't the right time. But we need to talk about it. We can't carry on like this. I want you and I want Toby.'

She swallowed and slipped down from the table, adjusting her clothing with shaking hands. He wanted Toby, and Toby wanted him—there was no doubt about that. It would be so simple to just let herself be persuaded. But was that the right decision? Toby needed a father and he adored Jed, but what about the risk involved?

What if Jed became bored with being 'Daddy'? What happened when Toby was demanding and whiny after a long day? What happened when he was muddy and cross and uncooperative, which all children were sometimes? What then? Would Jed regret his decision? And if he did, what would happen? Would he leave them or would he stay and become more and more bitter, like her father? Her father. She closed her eyes and swallowed. Dear God, she didn't know what to do. She knew what she wanted—she wanted Jed. But it wasn't that simple, was it?

She raised a shaking hand and brushed her tangled dark hair away from her face. She loved Jed so much, so very much, but part of her just wouldn't allow herself to let go.

'I—I don't think there'll ever be a right time...'

Because she just couldn't get past her childhood. However hard she tried to be rational, to tell herself that Jed wasn't like her father, the past was always there, taunting her, reminding her that she would be taking a huge risk with Toby's happiness. And her own.

He gave a short laugh and turned to face her, his dark eyes burning into hers. 'Oh, believe me, there will be a right time, Brooke. There is no way you and I can live on the same planet and not rip each other's clothes off.'

She swallowed hard, her eyes flickering shyly over his very male chest, exposed since she'd all but torn his shirt off. Dark hair covered the smooth swell of muscle and her fingers tingled with need. She wanted to touch him so badly.

'Jed—we can't.' How could she? How could she put her past behind her and expose herself and her child to possible hurt? How could she trust him to be able to tell the difference between wanting her and wanting Toby? She knew how much he loved his son—

He closed his eyes and gave a resigned sigh. 'It's getting late and now is not the time to start a heavy conversation.

But don't think that lets you off the hook. There will be other occasions.'

Would there? Unless she could deal with the memories of her childhood she didn't see how things could ever change. What was the point of more conversation when the problem was buried deep inside herself? The truth was her love for Jed was blocked by images of what her father had done to her, to her mother—images so strong they threatened to prevent her from ever following her heart.

CHAPTER EIGHT

FORTUNATELY the new senior registrar, Brian Wells, had started his post and Ken, the SHO, was improving after a spell of close supervision, so Brooke saw very little of Jed for the next few days.

Five days after she'd moved into Jed's house, there was a call from Sean Nicholson in A and E to say that he had a thirteen-year-old girl with abdominal pain.

'He wanted Jed, but he's doing a gynae list this afternoon,' Gill said with a frown. 'I've bleeped Brian and he's going to nip down to A and E. Will you meet him down there? Sounds like he might need moral support.'

'Why's Sean calling us?' Brooke asked, tucking her pen back into her pocket and pressing the button for the lift.

Gill pulled a face. 'He thinks she's in labour.'

Brooke's eyes widened. 'At thirteen?'

'Well, Sean's the best A and E consultant anyone has ever seen, so if he thinks the girl is in labour then I'm willing to bet she is,' Gill said briskly. 'Go down, assess her with Brian and get her up here if you've got time. If it's her first baby—and surely it must be at her age—I'm sure you will have time. In the meantime, Suzie and I will get one of the birthing rooms nice and cosy. I suspect she'll need a lot of TLC.'

Gill was right. Brooke winced as she approached A and E and heard the terrified screams coming from their trolley bay. She arrived at the same time as Brian, who acknowledged her with a friendly nod. Brian Wells was a nice chap and very competent, if rather staid. He didn't necessarily have Jed's extraordinary flair and talent, but he was good at his job nonetheless and would undoubtedly be an asset to the department.

Sean grabbed them both before they went behind the curtain, and gestured towards the small office in the trolley bay.

'She's thirteen. Obese, unfortunately, which is why she's managed to conceal the pregnancy, and the poor kid is absolutely terrified. Her mother is with her and I haven't spoken to her yet because I wanted you guys to confirm the gestation.'

Brian raised an eyebrow. 'You're sure she's pregnant?'

Brooke winced and held her breath, waiting for Sean to cut him down to size. The A and E consultant wasn't renowned for his patience and didn't usually take kindly to having his diagnosis questioned.

'Well, I certainly don't claim to be much of an obstetrician but I do recognise the sound of a foetal heart when I hear one,' Sean said dryly, handing the records over and pocketing his pen. 'But just for the sake of completeness one of the nurses has just gone to do a pregnancy test.'

'But she's only thirteen—she can't be pregnant.' Brian looked stunned and Brooke smothered a grin. The new senior reg had obviously led a very sheltered existence.

'You can break the news to the mother, Brian,' she muttered, noticing Sean's eyes gleam with unholy laughter as he appreciated the impact that her words would have on the SR. 'Shall we see the girl first?'

'Oh, of course.' Brian Wells looked flustered but straightened his glasses and peered at Sean. 'Where is she?'

Sean lifted an eyebrow as another scream echoed around the whole department. 'You need directions?'

Deciding that one of Sean's acid comments wasn't far round the corner, Brooke gave him a smile of thanks and walked briskly towards the side room in the trolley bay, hoping that Brian would follow her. He did and she slipped into the room and smiled at the terrified girl who was clinging to the sides of the trolley, her blonde hair limp and tangled.

Brooke took a swift look at her chart for the name. 'Hello, Carly. I'm Brooke and I'm a...nurse.' She didn't want to say that she was a midwife at this stage. 'What's been happening to you, sweetheart?'

The girl looked so young she would barely have passed for thirteen, and Brooke felt a pang of sympathy for her, and also for her mother who was looking equally terrified.

'I've had these pains for hours now.' Carly sobbed and writhed on the trolley. 'They're getting worse and worse.'

Brooke exchanged a quick look with Brian and took Carly's hand firmly in hers. 'Is the pain there all time?'

Carly shook her head, her breath coming in sobs. 'No. It comes and goes and it's terrible—*Ooh!*'

She screamed in panic and wriggled and thumped the sides of the trolley while Brooke stroked her hair and tried to soothe her quietly. Once the contraction was over she turned to Brian.

'We need to get her upstairs and give the poor thing something for pain. Let's just quickly examine her to get some idea of what's going on.'

She spoke obliquely so that Carly's mother wouldn't understand what was going on. Until they had all the information, there was no point in talking to her.

'Mrs Baxter, could I ask you to wait outside for just a moment?' Brooke ushered the older lady out of the room and then came back in to help Brian. He examined the girl thoroughly with Brooke as chaperone and then they left the side room to confer.

'Well?' Brooke frowned up at him and he let out a deep breath.

'Seven centimetres.' He looked staggered. 'I can't believe it. I was hoping Dr Nicholson might be wrong.'

'Sean Nicholson is never wrong about anything,' Brooke told him wryly, taking a deep breath and bracing herself for a difficult task. 'OK, we need to get her upstairs. And we need to tell the mother.'

Brian looked uncomfortable. 'I've never actually come

across a case like this before. She's under age. It's actually a criminal offence. The police should be told—'

'I don't think that's the main issue here,' Brooke pointed out gently, hoping they hadn't misjudged the man. 'That girl is going to have a baby, Dr Wells, sooner rather than later. I think we need to prepare her and her mother and worry about the ethics later.'

'I'd feel more comfortable talking to Mr Matthews about it,' Brian said briskly, glancing at his watch.

Which left her with the job he didn't want. With a wry smile Brooke sighed and accepted the inevitable.

'Fine. You do that. I'll talk to Carly and her mother.'

Relieved to have offloaded such an onerous task, Brian strode out of A and E and Brooke rolled her eyes. Maybe he wasn't such an asset after all. Or maybe Jed was just so good they'd all been spoiled.

She drew Mrs Baxter back into the room and quietly and tactfully explained that Carly was in labour, her whole attitude calm and non-judgemental as the mother exploded in shock and distress.

'But she's only thirteen! You must be mistaken!'

Brooke took a deep breath and braced herself. 'We're not mistaken, Mrs Baxter.'

The woman stared at her daughter in horror and shook her head. 'Carly, no! Tell me it can't be true.'

Carly started to sob hysterically and Brooke slipped an arm round the terrified girl, her voice soothing.

'There, sweetheart, don't panic. Your mum isn't really angry, she's just had a shock.' Brooke shot Mrs Baxter a warning glance. Whatever she thought of her daughter, Carly was still a child, and a very young one at that. She needed her mother's support, and if necessary Brooke was ready to point that out to her in no uncertain terms. There was no way she was going to let someone else suffer parental rejection if it could be helped.

'Who was it? That Harper boy, I expect. Well, I'll kill him—was it that Harper boy?' Mrs Baxter glared at her daughter, her fists clenched, and Brooke immediately took her arm and led her firmly outside.

'We're taking Carly up to the labour ward now, Mrs Baxter. She needs your support, not your recriminations. If you're not able to give it then I suggest you stay outside the room.'

Mrs Baxter glared at her angrily. 'Don't you dare tell me what I can and can't do!'

'On the contrary, unless you're supporting your daughter, Brooke is quite within her rights to ask you to leave.' Jed's firm voice came from behind them and Brooke turned in relief.

'Mr Matthews, we need to get Carly up to the labour ward. I'll phone a porter.'

'Forget the porter, I'll help you.' He gave Mrs Baxter a steady look. 'I realise that this has come as a shock to you, but your daughter needs you. I think you should consider her needs first and then worry about everything else later.'

Mrs Baxter huffed angrily. 'You wouldn't be so complacent if she was your daughter!'

Jed paused in the doorway of the room. 'I don't have a daughter, Mrs Baxter, but I do have a son, and I know that whatever he does in life, whatever mistakes he makes, I will still love him and be there for him. I'm sure that you feel the same way about Carly.'

Brooke felt a rush of admiration. He always seemed to know just the right thing to say in any situation.

Mrs Baxter took several deep breaths and winced as Carly screamed again. Then she marched off down the corridor towards the exit of A and E.

'Mum, no!' Carly's sobs doubled as she saw her mother disappearing. 'Mum, I'm sorry. Oh, the pain—help! I'm dying, *I'M DYING!*'

Jed watched Mrs Baxter go and muttered something unrepeatable under his breath, before turning his attention back to Carly.

'She needs pain relief, poor kid. Let's move her fast,' he

said quietly, his large hand smoothing the girl's hair. 'All right, sweetheart. Take a deep breath and we'll have you straight in a minute.'

Fifteen minutes later Jed had examined her thoroughly and declared everything fine.

'What happens now?' Carly asked, her face white with panic and distress as she glanced at the ever-increasing number of people around her bed.

Jed followed her glance and frowned. 'How on earth did we manage to accumulate this much of an audience? OK, everyone out except Brooke, please.'

He turned back to Carly, settling himself on the bed next to her, his strong hand covering hers. 'Everyone around here gets a bit over-excited when a baby is about to be born. It's a very special event, sweetheart.'

Carly shook her head from side to side, her breathing still erratic. 'No. No! I don't want a baby. I'm scared—help me!'

Her body convulsed with sobs again and Jed looked at Brooke, for once out of his depth. 'You try.'

Brooke followed her instincts and did what seemed right. She scooped the sobbing teenager into her arms and held her tightly, murmuring soothing words in a soft voice while she stroked her hair.

Over her head Jed raised his brows and waited, both of them hoping that some physical comfort might calm the child down. It did. Soon the sobs lessened but Carly didn't move, still clinging tightly to Brooke even when a contraction ripped through her plump frame, causing more howls.

Jed frowned and looked at Brooke, his voice soft. 'What do you reckon? Epidural?'

Brooke pulled a face. 'She just needs calming down. How about the pool? Gill was going to get one of the birthing rooms ready. It might do the trick.'

Jed looked at the exhausted girl and shrugged. 'Well, there's no reason why she shouldn't have a normal delivery and I certainly don't want to intervene unless I have to. We could give the pool a try, but isn't she a bit beyond the touch of aromatherapy oils and candles?'

'You'd be surprised.' Brooke shifted slightly so that she could look at Carly. 'Carly? It won't be long until you have your baby and you're very tense at the moment. We're going to take you through to the next room and put you in a lovely warm bath with some nice smellies and candles. And then you and I are going to have a lovely, cosy chat, like sisters.'

Carly looked at her and nodded, her eyes dull with pain, and without further ado Jed and Brooke wheeled her into the next room and helped her into the water.

'I'm going to leave you to it,' Jed said quietly. 'I think the fewer people the better, and my new senior reg wants to talk to me about the correct course of action in certain circumstances.'

He rolled his eyes expressively, and in spite of the tension Brooke smothered a grin. Unless she was mistaken, Brian Wells was about to receive the sharp end of Jed's tongue.

Supported by the water, Carly calmed down significantly and Brooke lit the candles and put some soft music on the CD player. Suddenly the room wasn't part of a hospital any more, but was somewhere cosy and safe, somewhere that any woman would want to give birth. One of the midwives had even found a few soft toys and had piled them on the bed for Carly. Brooke sighed as she looked at them. She was ready to bet that Carly hadn't moved beyond the stuffed-toy stage herself yet.

She knelt down by the pool and checked the baby's heart with the underwater ultrasound, satisfied with what she heard. 'Oh, listen to that, Carly! Can you hear the little heart?'

She tried to involve the girl, to work up some excitement, but Carly looked more scared than ever. 'It's really going to happen, isn't it?'

'It certainly is,' Brooke said with a gentle smile. 'Did you really not know you were pregnant?'

Carly looked sheepish. 'Well, I did wonder, but we only did it once…'

Brooke bit her lip. 'It only takes the once, Carly.'

'Well, I know that now, don't I?' Carly dipped further under the water, her eyes closed. 'Oh, this feels brill. I couldn't have told my mum, you know. She'd have gone off the deep end, like she just did.'

'It was just the shock, Carly,' Brooke soothed, 'She'll come round.'

'She won't forgive me.' Carly's voice was a thin whisper and Brooke gritted her teeth. If she could find Mrs Baxter she'd throttle her. She ought to be here with Carly, supporting her child through thick and thin.

'Just try and relax, Carly. Feel the water around you…' Brooke stroked the girl's shoulders and Carly breathed in deeply.

'That's such a nice smell—what is it?'

'Aromatherapy oils,' Brooke murmured, shifting her position with a wince as Carly braced herself for another contraction.

Calmly and patiently Brooke helped her with her breathing, teaching her quickly the best way to ride the pain and explaining what her young body was trying to do.

'Don't fight it, Carly.' She stroked the matted hair gently, using touch as a comfort. 'Your body is an amazing thing. It's pushing this baby out by itself and you've got to help it.'

Quietly she used visualisation techniques to help Carly relax and get her into a more positive frame of mind, and soon Carly was coping well with each contraction, her young face determined and almost calm.

'Has anyone ever told you you're a genius?' Jed slid quietly back into the room and watched with open admiration in his face as Brooke worked with the girl, helping her encourage her body to do what it was designed for.

'Don't tell her that, she'll expect a pay rise,' Gill said dryly from the doorway. 'Brooke, I'll stay with Carly for a few minutes—there's someone who wants to talk to you in the staffroom.'

'No!' Carly's expression was one of utter panic. 'I don't want her to leave me. Please, let her stay...'

Gill squatted down by the pool, her eyes kind. 'There, pet, she'll only be gone a minute and I'll stay here with you until she comes back.'

Brooke frowned and straightened, her eyes questioning Gill, and then understanding dawned and she realised it must be Carly's mother. Her chin lifted angrily and Jed put a restraining hand on her arm, his eyes flashing a warning.

'Maybe you're not the best person to do this,' he muttered softly, glancing warily at Gill who obviously didn't know Brooke's history.

'On the contrary, Jed, I'm exactly the right person.' She shook off his hand and stooped to give Carly a big hug. 'You are the bravest, most brilliant mum-to-be we've ever had on this unit, so keep it up. I'll be back in ten minutes.'

'Hopefully with your mother,' she muttered to herself as she left the room and strode towards the staffroom, her heart racing.

Mrs Baxter was standing facing the door, her hands twisting together as she waited for Brooke.

'How is she?' She took a step forward, her face working, and Brooke gave her a cool look.

'Considering she's barely thirteen years old and she's currently going through one of life's most painful experiences alone and without support, she's holding out marvellously.' Brooke's eyes flashed but her words were controlled and professional. 'In the past few hours your daughter has learned that she's to be a parent, has coped with the agonies of an unsupported labour and has been rejected by her own mother. All pretty stressful, really.'

Mrs Baxter made a distressed sound. 'I haven't rejected her—but she's made me so ashamed. I need time to get used to the idea—'

'You haven't got time,' Brooke said frankly, her dark

eyes cool but not entirely unsympathetic. 'It's not that I don't understand that you've had a terrible shock, Mrs Baxter, but the truth is, it's happened! Nothing can undo that, but by rejecting your daughter when she really, really needs her mum, you could do irreparable harm. I know that you need time to adjust, but Carly has needs too, and hers are immediate and she's just a child. She needs her mother.'

Mrs Baxter closed her eyes. 'What on earth are people going to say?'

Brooke hesitated and then decided that she just had to speak her mind. 'I hope they'll say that you stood by your daughter through thick and thin, showing her by example what good parenting is all about. I hope they'll say that, although you were upset and embarrassed about the whole thing, you put Carly's needs above your own and gave her the very best support you possibly could. I hope they'll say that when the Baxters are in trouble, they stick together like glue.'

Mrs Baxter stared at her, her face working, and then she burst into tears, rummaging up her sleeve for a tissue. 'I'm sorry. You're right, of course, it's just so hard.'

Brooke bit her lip. She actually had a lot of sympathy for the mother but Carly's needs were paramount in her opinion. 'Do you love your daughter, Mrs Baxter?'

'Well, of course I do!' Mrs Baxter looked horrified. 'Just because I'm angry at the moment doesn't mean I don't love her.'

Brooke gave her a crooked smile and opened the door. 'Well, in that case I suggest you go and tell her that, and give her a bit of motherly love. So far she's only had me cuddling her and I'm a total stranger. She needs her mother.'

Mrs Baxter hesitated and then took a deep breath and nodded. 'Yes. Of course I'll go to her. Take me, will you?'

Without wasting any more time, Brooke hurried her down the corridor and into the birthing room.

'Mum?' Carly was clutching Gill's hand and panting while Jed scribbled something in the notes.

'Sweetheart!' Mrs Baxter crossed the room in an undignified rush, tears on her face. 'Mummy's here, pet...'

With that she folded the girl in her arms, ignoring the fact that she was wet from the pool, and Brooke swallowed back a lump in her throat. Thank goodness for that!

'Mum, I'm sorry.' Carly's face was blotched. 'So sorry.'

'Don't you worry, pet,' her mother said softly. 'We'll work it out together, I promise. Now, then, how are the pains?'

Carly gave a weak smile. 'Better now I'm in the water. I love it in here. I don't want to get out. Do I have to get out when the baby's born?'

'I don't know, darling.' Mrs Baxter looked at Brooke anxiously. 'Does she? Is it safe being in the pool? In my day we didn't have anything like this. Is it OK for her to stay in?'

'It's fine.' Brooke nodded quickly and checked the baby's heart again before examining Carly. 'She's quite safe in the water. If we're at all worried we'll get her out but, to be honest, she's a million times more relaxed since she climbed in there and a great deal calmer.'

'Has she had something for the pain?' Mrs Baxter glanced at them and Jed came forward, his handsome face serious.

'We're using the water as a form of pain relief, Mrs Baxter. The warmth is very relaxing and she can move around easily. Many pregnant women find it all the pain relief they need. If Carly needs something more or wants to come out of the water, that's fine. We'll deal with it when the time comes.'

'We never had anything like that when I was expecting,' Mrs Baxter murmured, and Jed smiled.

'Well, it certainly wasn't the norm in hospitals until fairly recently, and even now lots of hospitals don't have birthing pools, but water therapy has been used for years as a muscle relaxant.'

'I can't think why I like it so much,' Carly mumbled. 'I hate swimming.'

Brooke smiled. 'Well, funnily enough, underwater births were pioneered by a Russian swimming instructor—but I don't think pregnant women were really expected to swim very far!'

'It's brilliant, Mum, and I don't feel so fat and horrible in the water. Ooh...' Carly started to groan again and Brooke encouraged her to breathe properly, checking the baby's heart again.

'That all sounds fine, Carly.'

Jed walked towards the door. 'I'll leave you to it, but I'd like to be here when she delivers.'

Brooke nodded, knowing that he wanted to be around in case anything went wrong. He was that sort of man. He cared enough to make sure that Carly wasn't frightened any more than she already had been.

An hour later Carly became very restless and retched repeatedly. Her mother stroked her hair and looked at Brooke in panic.

'She's fine,' Brooke murmured, ringing the buzzer for some back-up. 'She's in what we call transition. She'll be ready to push in a minute.'

Minutes later Jed slipped into the room with Gill close behind him, and together they got everything ready for an imminent delivery, leaving Brooke to deal with Carly.

'Concentrate on your body, Carly,' she urged. 'Try and imagine the baby moving down. Deep breath in—that's great—and again. See it in your mind, feel it with your body...'

Gently she examined Carly and then took the girl's hand and moved it between her legs. 'Feel that.'

Carly's eyes widened. 'What is it?'

'Your baby's head,' Brooke told her with an excited smile. 'Keep your hand there and tell me what you feel.'

Carly groaned as another pain came and then gasped. 'Oh! I felt it push into my hand. Oh, Mum!'

'Little pants now, Carly,' Brooke instructed, reaching

down to guide the baby out. 'That's it. Well done... Perfect...'

The baby flipped out easily and Brooke lifted it out of the water into Carly's arms, tears clogging her own eyes as she saw the stunned amazement and delight on the young girl's face.

'Oh, Mum!' Tears poured down Carly's cheeks and Brooke heard Gill clear her throat behind her.

'You have a son, Carly.' Her own voice was husky and more than a little shaky. 'Congratulations, sweetheart.'

'He's not crying.' Mrs Baxter looked at them anxiously. 'Aren't you meant to tip him upside down and slap him?'

Jed laughed. 'I don't think he'd be very pleased if I did that!' Moving closer to them, his expression sobered. 'Seriously, Mrs Baxter, we find that babies born in the water often don't cry. It seems to be a more gentle introduction to the world for them, but look at him. He's pink and healthy and breathing beautifully.'

'He's beautiful, Mum. Look at him.' Carly was sobbing now, holding the baby against her and stroking his wrinkled skin. 'Don't make me give him away. Please, Mum. Don't make me give him away. He's mine.'

Mrs Baxter shook her head, barely able to speak for the emotion of it all. 'No, love. How can we ever give him away?' Her eyes met Brooke's and were full of gratitude and peace. 'He's family.'

'Well, thank goodness we don't go through an emotional experience like that every day of the week,' Gill said briskly, flicking on the kettle and spooning coffee into three mugs. 'I'd be a wreck.'

'You are a wreck, Sister.' Jed leaned his powerful shoulders against the wall and laughed openly. 'Your hair is somewhat ruffled and your mascara has run.'

Gill flapped a hand and glared at him. 'Get away with you! You're no gentleman, Jed Matthews! You're not meant to notice that a lady is in emotional distress.'

'Not notice?' His blue eyes flashed wickedly. 'Gill, you weren't so much distressed as emotionally incontinent in there—how could I possibly not notice?'

Brooke grinned. 'Oh, and you were totally immune, I suppose, Mr-ice-cool-I-never-show-any-emotions Matthews?'

'Oh, totally,' Jed said gravely, straightening and making for one of the chairs. 'Didn't affect me at all.'

'So why were your eyelashes stuck together when her mother made that speech about families?' Brooke's tone was teasing and Jed's eyes laughed into hers.

'Er, could it have been the steam from the birthing pool?'

'No, it could not!' Brooke and Gill laughed together and Gill handed him a coffee.

'Here we are, drink this—it'll soothe your nerves. And for the record, our pool doesn't steam—certainly not enough to make someone's eyelashes wet.'

'OK—I admit it!' Jed sat back in his chair and shook his head slowly. 'I'm a softy underneath. But you must admit that was a pretty moving experience.'

'It was amazing,' Gill said gruffly, handing round the biscuits and helping herself to two. 'And you were brilliant, Brooke. Absolutely brilliant. What on earth did you say to the woman?'

Brooke exchanged glances with Jed and gave an embarrassed smile. 'Nothing much.'

'Oh, I'll bet...' Jed breathed, draining his coffee and making for the door. 'I'm off back to Gynae to see what my team is up to and to check that Brian Wells hasn't called the police.'

'The police?' Gill raised her eyebrows. 'Why would he do that?'

'He thought it might have been his responsibility,' Jed murmured dryly, 'but I was able to gently persuade him that it wasn't.'

Brooke frowned. 'Do you think the mother will contact the police?'

Jed shrugged. 'I don't know. She's certainly entitled to, but it's not anything to do with us. All the same, we probably ought to give Social Services a ring. The family need some support, in the early days at least.'

'I'll ring them,' Gill said, 'and the health visitor as well.'

'Good stuff.' Jed opened the door and then paused. 'Oh, and by the way, Brooke, I'll be late tonight. I'm giving a lecture on antepartum haemorrhage. You'd better eat without me.'

Without waiting for her reply, Jed left the room, leaving Brooke, scarlet-faced and inwardly cursing.

'Well, that was tactful of him.' Gill laughed, handing Brooke another biscuit. 'Bite on that, Brooke, dear. You can pretend it's his ankle and you're a Jack Russell.'

Brooke refused the biscuit and shook her head slowly. 'It isn't what you think...'

'It isn't my business to think anything, dear,' Gill said briskly. 'Your private life is entirely your own affair. But I would say one thing...'

Brooke looked at her warily. 'What?'

'I know how very independent you are, and that's a very admirable quality.' Gill's voice was calm and matter-of-fact. 'But if you let a man like that slip through your fingers you'll be making the biggest mistake of your life.'

Brooke hesitated. 'It's complicated...'

'Love often is.' Gill stood up and adjusted her belt, before pacing over to the mirror and scowling at her reflection. 'Dear me, the man's right! I look like a panda!'

She wiped the mascara from under her eyes and turned back to Brooke, her expression kind.

'Don't let things be complicated, dear. Follow your instincts and don't spend your life erecting obstacles to happiness.'

Brooke watched as she left the room, her heart thudding. Was Gill right? Should she follow her instincts? If she did that then she had no doubt at all where her instincts would lead. She loved Jed and all she really wanted was to be with him. In every sense.

But did she dare? Brooke closed her eyes and took a deep breath. Did she really dare expose her feelings like that and take the risk that he'd turn out to be like her father?

She opened her eyes and stared around the cluttered staff-room. Where was she going in her life? What was she doing? Turning down her one chance at happiness because she was too scared to trust Jed's feelings. But maybe he *did* care for her. Maybe it *was* her he wanted and not just Toby.

She bit her lip and sorted through her tangled thoughts. She loved him so much. So very much.

Later that afternoon there was an unusual lull on the labour ward and Brooke popped up to the special care baby unit to visit Linda's baby, who had been delivered after the car crash. It had been five weeks since that awful night and everyone was amazed by how well the baby had done.

'He's given us some nasty moments, if I'm honest, but he seems determined to hang on and he's doing well now.' Sita Patel smiled down at her little charge in the incubator and watched while one of the nurses fiddled with a monitor.

'I can't believe he's still with us. When I came up a few weeks ago it was touch and go.' Brooke stared down at the tiny scrap and her heart twisted.

'Jed's been checking up on her, too.' Sita looked at her curiously. 'Of course, you were with him when Linda had the accident, weren't you?'

Brooke gave a stiff smile. Did the whole hospital know? 'Well, yes...'

'She was jolly lucky you were the ones who found her,' Sita said, fiddling with one of the monitors again.

'How is Linda?'

'Well, she's been discharged now obviously,' Sita told her, 'but she comes in every day and stays for as long as she can. She's got five-year-old twins at home so it's not easy for her.'

'Poor lady. Still, we'll keep our finger crossed.'

Remembering that Jed was going to be late and that Toby was staying at a friend's for the first time, Brooke planned a relaxing evening with a long bath and a book.

It was late and she'd just climbed out of the bath and was drying her hair when she was suddenly aware that she wasn't alone.

Her heart in her mouth, she turned with a gasp and then sagged with relief when she saw Jed standing in the doorway, his powerful legs planted firmly apart and those blue eyes roving hungrily over her body.

'Sorry. I didn't mean to scare you.' His voice was gruff and he threw her a lopsided, apologetic grin as he turned to go. 'I'll go and fix us some drinks. Join me when you're ready.'

'Wait, Jed!' Why was her voice so husky and why were her hands shaking so badly? How did you tell a man that you wanted him without looking like a shameless hussy? Because that was the truth, she realised suddenly. She wanted him with her whole heart and every fibre of her being.

'What?' Jed paused and glanced back briefly, his face looking taut and strained. Why was he in such a hurry to leave? She watched him closely, noticing his increased breathing and the snug fit of his trousers.

With a gentle, enticing smile that was totally feminine she walked towards him.

'I don't think I want a drink, Jed.'

He stiffened and watched her approach, his blue eyes wary. 'Fair enough, I'll have—'

'Kiss me.' Brooke felt her heart thump as he stared at her, stunned. Had he heard her? Was he going to refuse? 'Kiss me, Jed.'

He shook his head slowly, his hard jaw rigid with tension. 'I can't, Brooke. If I touch you, I make love to you—it's as simple as that.' He took a deep breath and rubbed his forehead with long fingers. 'I don't think there are any half-measures for you and I, sweetheart. I can't just kiss you and then let you go.'

Brooke swallowed hard, her nerve failing. 'I don't want you to let me go.'

His hand dropped to his side and he looked at her questioningly, his blue eyes narrowed.

She tried again, for the last time. 'Kiss me, Jed. Please?'

CHAPTER NINE

JED'S hands were clenched by his sides, and he seemed to struggle to find his voice.

'Toby?'

'He's staying at a friend's tonight. It's a sleepover party.'

For a long moment he just stared at Brooke, digesting what she'd said, and then he crossed the room slowly, stopping just in front of her.

'Brooke?'

Her heart fluttering wildly, she placed her slim fingers on his broad chest, feeling the smooth curve of muscle underneath the soft fabric of his shirt.

'Are you going to stand there talking all night, Jed, or are you—'

His hands cupped her face roughly and his mouth prevented her from uttering the rest of her sentence, possessing hers with a passion that made her knees weaken. Without lifting his mouth, he dropped one hand to the small of her back, holding her firmly against his hard body as he continued to kiss her as if it might be the last time they were able to touch.

Desperate for more, her mouth opened under his and his tongue seduced hers, coaxing and demanding until she was sobbing with need.

Dimly she felt a sharp tug as he released the towel, and then she was naked in his arms, the warmth from his hands making her whole body shiver with reaction as he stroked and held her.

'Jed, please...'

Her whole body was on fire with need, she could barely stand and hardly breathe and she wanted him so badly she didn't think she could wait another moment. It had been so many years…

'Not here.' With a rough groan Jed dragged his mouth away from hers and scooped her into his arms, striding down the landing and shouldering his way into the master bedroom at the back of the house.

Without breaking contact, he laid her on the bed and his mouth found hers again, biting and nibbling her lips until she was twisting in a frenzy of desire beneath his powerful body.

Without lifting his mouth from hers, he wrenched off his tie and fumbled with the buttons of his shirt, breathing heavily as she lifted her hands to help him.

The shirt fell to the floor, forgotten, and Brooke slid her hands over his hard shoulders, loving the silken feel of his warm flesh, incredibly aware of just how strong this man was.

Her hands trailed slowly downwards, through the dark hair covering his chest and down until her fingers met the waistband of his trousers.

His eyes fierce with need, Jed lifted his head and stared down at her, his breathing rapid and unsteady.

'I want you so much—so much.' With a groan he planted hot, open-mouthed kisses down her neck, his tongue trailing over the curve of her breast and gently teasing the dusky rose of one nipple.

With a cry she arched towards him and he took her in his mouth, his teeth and tongue working a magic that pulled and twisted her insides until she was writhing beneath him.

'Please, Jed—now…' She tugged uselessly at his zip, feeling the thickness of his arousal through the fabric of his trousers. Now. Now. She wanted him now.

'Patience,' he growled, his own hand shaking as he dealt with the zip and let her slide his trousers down his hard, very muscular thighs. With one swift movement he was as naked as she was, and her throat dried as she looked at him properly for the first time.

They hadn't switched on any lights on the night of the Christmas Ball and she'd never really seen Jed properly, but now, illuminated by the soft light from the landing, her eyes roved over his powerful physique and her cheeks heated slightly.

'What's the matter?' He slowed the pace, stroking her cheek with a gentle finger, the look in his blue eyes warm and intimate. 'We've done this before, sweetheart, remember? You know I'd never hurt you.'

'I know that...' Suddenly Brooke felt ridiculously shy and he gave her a wicked grin and the sexiest wink she'd ever received.

'Come here.' He pulled her towards him and lowered his mouth, kissing her with deliberate intimacy, driving her wild with his tongue and hands until all she could think about was the hot, burning sensation in the pit of her stomach which only this man could cure.

Forgetting her shyness, she smoothed her hands over his heated flesh, needing to touch him as he was touching her. As her hands moved downwards she felt his breath catch and his body tremble with reaction.

There was a brief pause as he remembered to protect her and then he gave a rough exclamation and slipped a hand under her bottom, drawing her towards him. Their breath mingled and her eyes locked with his as he entered her with one deep thrust, their mutual desperation a primitive force that swept them along in its path.

There was no holding back, no question of control. Six years without each other had left them both starving for the touch of the other. Brooke felt him drive into her, filling her completely with each thrust, his powerful male body dominating and possessing her.

'I love you...' His voice fractured slightly as they moved together, and she sobbed his name, feeling her body spiralling out of control and bursting with the intensity of feeling that consumed her.

At the same time he stiffened, the spasms contracting his

body as he cried out her name and then dropped his head on her shoulder, his breathing erratic. For what seemed like ages he held her like that, and then he lifted his dark head.

'God, Brooke...' The expression in his blue eyes was stunned. 'Tell me I didn't hurt you, sweetheart.'

She gave him a shy smile and stroked his damp forehead with the tips of her fingers.

'You didn't hurt me. Couldn't you tell?'

He closed his eyes briefly and dropped a gentle kiss on her mouth. 'I don't know what you do to me but it's scary.'

She stared into his eyes, longing for him to tell her again that he loved her, but he didn't. Instead, he gave a groan and muttered that he was too heavy for her, shifting his body across the bed and curling her into his side.

Brooke placed a hand on his hard chest, feeling his heartbeat racing under her fingertips. It was just the circumstances, she told herself, trying not to feel disappointed. She knew he didn't love her really. All men probably said things like that when they made love. She mustn't read anything into it.

Determined not to spoil the moment, she closed her eyes, loving the male smell of him that tantalised her senses, loving how safe it made her feel, feeling the hard muscle of his arm under her cheek. Her hand crept down his body and he gave a low murmur of protest, turning his head so that his eyes gleamed gently into hers.

'I was letting you rest...'

It had been six years! She didn't want to rest.

Her mouth curved into a womanly smile and in one swift movement she was sitting astride him, his hands holding the soft curve of her bottom.

'Never look at me like that unless you mean it,' he said gruffly, and she lowered her lids slightly, her dark eyes teasing.

'I mean it, Mr Matthews.'

His deep breath in was decidedly unsteady. 'Well, in that case...'

* * *

When Brooke awoke it was morning and she was alone in the bed. She sat up, raked her tangled dark hair away from her face and then heard clattering in the kitchen. Was he going to surprise her with breakfast? She smiled sleepily. Maybe she'd surprise him first.

Padding across the landing in her bare feet, she started to walk down the stairs but froze as she heard the doorbell ring.

Who on earth was calling at this hour? Retreating to the top of the stairs, she hovered anxiously, hoping there wasn't a problem with Toby. Had he been homesick? Had something happened? No, of course not. They would have phoned if there'd been a problem.

'Jed, I need to talk to you.' The caller was male and Brooke could just make out Jed's muttered response.

'Tom, this isn't a good time.'

It was Tom?

About to retreat to the bedroom and leave them to have their conversation in private, Brooke froze as Tom mentioned her name.

'That is none of your business, little brother.' Whatever Tom had said had obviously angered Jed, but Tom wasn't giving an inch, his voice rising.

'You have to marry her, Jed!'

'Keep out of it, Tom!' Jed's voice was a threatening growl and the front door opened as Tom obviously prepared to make his escape.

'You have no choice and you know it! Why not just admit that this time you've been well and truly caught?'

Brooke didn't wait to hear Jed's reply but instead dashed along the landing to the sanctuary of her own room, bolting the door behind her.

Her heart thumped uncomfortably and she closed her eyes.

No choice?

Why did Tom think that Jed had no choice but to marry her?

She gave a moan of panic. The answer was as clear as

day. Because, like the rest of his family, he knew about Toby.

Was that why Jed was pursuing their relationship? Was he responding to pressure from his family as well as his own sense of responsibility? Obviously his family *were* putting pressure on him—she'd just heard the evidence with her own ears. They were telling him he had to marry her.

Shaking with emotion, she dressed, hardly noticing what she was wearing as she dragged her clothes on haphazardly. The rest of her clothes she stuffed into her suitcase, along with the other bits and pieces she'd retrieved from her house. She had to get away from him as fast as possible.

Tonight when she'd finished her shift she'd go straight home to her cottage, and she and Toby would just have to live in it as it was until she had time to get some quotes and arrange for the work to be done.

At least it was Saturday and Toby was spending the day with his friend. She was due to pick him up on her way home from work—

'Brooke—are you there, sweetheart?' Jed's voice came through the door, strong and concerned. 'Are you all right?'

'I'm fine.' Her voice was shaky. Dear God, what could she say to him? 'I'll be out in a moment.'

She saw the handle move and she closed her eyes, bracing herself for the inevitable.

'Why have you locked the door?' Puzzlement turned to anger as he rattled the door hard. 'Dammit, open this door, Brooke!'

'I want to be on my own, Jed.'

She could wait until he'd gone to work and then leave—

'Like hell you do!' His voice was raw as he thumped the door one more time. 'I will not leave you alone—not until you tell me what's happened. Don't do this to me again, Brooke! Don't shut me out.'

She swallowed down the lump in her throat, fighting the impulse to just open the door and fling herself in his arms. Who cared if he didn't really want to marry her? If he was only getting involved with her because of Toby? Who cared?

She sighed and lifted a shaking hand to her throat. She cared, because she didn't want that sort of relationship. It was obvious that they couldn't just have a fling. His family were determined to see him 'do the right thing'. Why else would Tom tell him that he had no choice but to marry her?

She loved Jed so much, so totally, that she couldn't let him get involved with her out of a sense of responsibility. He deserved better than that. But she knew that at the moment he wanted her and probably his hormones would cloud his thinking. She composed herself and lifted her chin. Which meant that it was up to her to convince him that she wasn't interested.

'Brooke, if you don't open this door now I'm going to break it down.' His tone left her in no doubt that he meant it and she rose to her feet and turned the key, stepping back as he slammed the door open and glared at her.

'What the hell is going on, Brooke?'

She flinched at the look in his eyes and backed away. 'Jed...'

'Don't look at me like that!' He frowned at her and raked long fingers through his dark hair. 'Don't back away from me. You know I would never, ever hurt you. I just want to know what's happened. I leave you curled up in my bed as contented as a kitten, and I come back upstairs with breakfast to find that you've locked yourself in your bedroom. I deserve an explanation.'

Brooke fought the almost overwhelming urge to touch him one last time. 'I— This isn't right Jed.'

His eyes narrowed. 'What isn't right?'

'Us.' She met his eyes bravely, hoping that she could be convincing. 'We shouldn't—it shouldn't have happened.'

'What shouldn't have happened?' There was a long silence while he looked at her and then he spoke, his voice lethally soft. 'Are you trying to tell me that we shouldn't have made love? If so, you're wasting your breath. It was totally right and you know it.'

'Maybe, at the time...' Her voice was little more than a croak and she dropped her gaze, unable to look him in the eye. 'But it was still a mistake.'

'Based on what?' His hard mouth was set in a grim line. 'Give me one very good reason why it was a mistake, Brooke.'

She took a deep breath and stared straight at him. 'Because I don't love you, Jed.'

There was a long silence while he looked at her, a muscle working in his dark jaw. He hadn't bothered to shave and he looked very male and very, very sexy.

'You don't love me.' He repeated her words flatly and turned and stared out of the window, his broad shoulders rigid with tension.

'That's right.' Her voice was amazingly steady in the circumstances. 'I thought I did but I don't.'

'I don't believe you.'

She swallowed, knowing just how astute this man was. 'I'm sorry, Jed, but it's true. I—I just don't feel the right way about you.'

The silence seemed to stretch into infinity and then finally he seemed to stir himself, turning and crossing the room towards the door, his mouth set in a grim line.

'Well, then, there's nothing more to be said, is there?' Suddenly he looked tired and defeated and she could barely control the tears as she remembered the warmth in his eyes when they'd made love. Why did this have to happen? Why?

'I'll finish packing my things,' she said huskily, and he gave a brief nod.

'Fine.' He turned to go and then paused. 'I'd still like to take Toby to my parents for the day tomorrow. I'll collect him in the morning and you can pick him up any time after lunch.'

With that he turned on his heel and walked towards his

bedroom, slamming the door behind him so that the whole house shook.

'You look awful.'

Brooke smiled wanly. 'Thanks, Gill. Thanks a bunch.'

'Anything I can do?'

Not unless she had a magic wand to wave over Jed to make him truly love her, Brooke thought glumly.

'No.' She turned on a bright smile that fooled no one. 'I'm fine. What's happening today, then?'

'Well, we're going to be busy,' Gill warned her, and Brooke rolled her eyes.

'When are we ever not busy?'

'True.' Gill checked the board and pulled a face. 'In fact, we're so busy I hardly know where to put you. The tricky one is likely to be the lady in 6—she's a forty-year-old primip and it's an IVF baby. Very precious baby. Very worried parents. Need I say more?'

Brooke gave a tired smile. 'I get the picture. Any problems?'

'Not so far.' Gill gathered up some notes and tucked them under her arm. 'She came in at about eight o'clock last night because her waters broke, but her contractions stopped so we sent her to the ward. Then they started again at about six o'clock this morning so they transferred her back up here for monitoring because she's so twitchy.'

'Fine. I'll get to it, then.' Brooke straightened her uniform and walked down the corridor towards Room 6.

The couple were both sitting on the bed, leafing through magazines together.

'Hello, I'm Brooke, and I'll be with you for the rest of the day.' Brooke smiled at them both and picked up the notes, checking the time of the last examination and quickly scanning the CTG trace that was stuffed into the notes.

'I'd hoped I might have had it by now,' the woman murmured, glancing anxiously at her husband. 'The suspense is almost too much to bear. I just want it to come.'

Brooke nodded sympathetically. 'I understand that, but nature takes its time, I'm afraid, especially with first babies.'

'But I'm so tired already.' The woman lifted a shaking hand to her head and Brooke could see the panic in her eyes.

'Carol—can I call you Carol? You've got a long way to go and it's important that you relax as much as possible. Has anyone talked to you about pain relief?'

'I said on my birth plan that I didn't want any.' She sniffed. 'I don't want to do anything that might harm this baby.'

Brooke settled herself on the bed, knowing that she had a lot of work to do if she was going to succeed in making this woman feel comfortable and relaxed.

'It's nice to draw up a birth plan, because it helps us to know what you feel strongly about, but once you're actually in labour sometimes it's best to forget all your preconceived ideas and just do what feels right.'

'I don't know what feels right any more.' Carol twisted her hands together and bit her lip. 'I'm just so terrified that something will be wrong.'

Brooke's voice was gentle. 'Why should something be wrong?'

'Because I want a baby so badly.' Carol's voice was barely a whisper and her husband slipped an arm around her shoulders. 'We've been trying for fourteen years, you know.'

Brooke felt her heart twist in sympathy and put her slim fingers over the other woman's hand. 'It will be fine, Carol—trust me.'

Carol shook her head. 'It's not that I don't trust you. I know that you're all brilliant here, everyone says so, but I just can't believe that this is going to happen to me at last. We had six attempts at IVF, and then we gave up because we ran out of money.'

Brooke was stunned. Six attempts must have cost them a

fortune. No wonder they'd run out of money. 'Didn't the health authority fund it?'

'The first one.' Carol gave a bitter laugh. 'After that you're on your own. We sold the car, gave up going out, didn't go on holidays—it was all worth it because I truly believed the IVF would work.'

Brooke swallowed, deeply touched by Carol's story. 'And did it work on the sixth attempt?'

'No.' Carol shook her head. 'When the sixth attempt failed I was so depressed I wanted to die. What was the point in carrying on if I couldn't have children? Everyone has children. Everywhere you look someone is pregnant, or wheeling a pram around.'

'I don't think that's true,' Brooke said softly. 'It just seems that way when you're desperate.'

'Yes, well, I was desperate.' Carol gave a short laugh and then winced and drew in a deep breath as a contraction started to build. For endless seconds she breathed and then she relaxed. 'Another one down. Where was I? Oh, yes, Bill and I even split up for a while because I was so convinced that he couldn't possibly want me if I couldn't give him children.'

The pain and love in her husband's eyes was clear to see and Brooke swallowed hard. Why was life so unfair? This lovely, lovely couple had obviously suffered so much.

'But you obviously weren't apart for long.'

Bill shook his head, taking up the story. 'I moved into a flat for a month to give Carol some space, but I missed her like crazy. I had a terrible job convincing her that I wanted her, with or without a baby.'

Carol squeezed his hand, her eyes filling. 'He was so great. He blew the last of our savings on a surprise holiday and we went to a luxury hotel and lazed on the beach for a week. We felt so much better at the end of it and decided that we were going to give IVF one more try and then give up and accept that we couldn't have children. So my sister lent me the money and we went ahead.'

Brooke shook her head in wonder. 'And it worked...'

'It worked.' Carol stroked her bump lovingly, her eyes filling. 'It was twins, you know, but I lost one at eight weeks.'

'I'm sorry,' Brooke said gruffly. 'No wonder you're so worried that something will go wrong.'

Carol nodded slowly. 'Yes. I just want it out now. I want to see it and keep it safe.'

'I understand that, Carol.' Brooke's eyes were gentle. 'But at the moment the baby is better off where he is. Would it reassure you more if you were connected to the monitor so that you can hear his heart?'

Carol looked at her and nodded. 'Yes. Yes, I think it would. I'm just so afraid that someone is going to miss something and I'm going to lose the baby.'

Brooke shook her head, an enormous lump in her throat. 'Carol, I swear to you that nothing is going to go wrong. I am going to be with you every step of the way and we'll do this together. We'll listen to that baby's heart as often as you like, we'll see how things go and I'll explain all the options. If at any time I am even slightly concerned then I'll call our consultant and he's a genius.'

'Is that Mr Matthews?'

'That's right.'

'I saw him in clinic and my infertility specialist said that I wouldn't find a better obstetrician than him anywhere in the country.'

'He's right.' Sadness ripped through Brooke but she forced herself to ignore her own pain. At the moment this woman's worries were a priority. 'Carol, this baby is going to be fine. Will you trust me?'

Carol smiled and nodded. 'Yes. I feel better, actually. Thanks for listening.'

'My privilege.' Brooke stood up and connected Carol to the machine, smiling as they heard the rapid thud of the baby's heart. 'Well, that's fine. What we'll do now is just check how he reacts to each contraction.'

Always a careful midwife, Brooke had never been so vigilant as she was with Carol. She checked everything repeatedly, helped Carol with her breathing and did everything she could to relax the couple.

She suggested the pool but Carol was adamant that it didn't appeal to her.

'I know it's illogical but I just can't help thinking that the baby shouldn't be in water.'

'That's fine, but your labour is going pretty slowly,' Brooke told her, trying not to make her anxious. 'We need to try and speed things up if we can or the baby might get tired. Could you get up and walk around a bit if Bill helps you?'

With a huge effort Carol manoeuvred her bulk off the bed and started to pace, with her husband supporting her.

Dave Richards, the infertility consultant, popped his head in halfway through the day to see how she was doing, and Brooke took the opportunity to leave the room and bleep Jed. She would have given anything to avoid him completely but she had a feeling that he was going to be needed.

He rang back immediately, his voice crisp and professional as he asked her questions about the woman.

'I'll come up and see her when I've finished clinic,' he said finally, after she'd told him the whole story. 'Hopefully she won't need any help, but you're right to play it safe. I'll have a word with Dave, too, before I see her.'

Replacing the receiver, Brooke walked back into the room and carried on encouraging Carol to move around and stay upright, helping her breathe as the contractions became stronger and closer together.

It was three o'clock when Jed arrived, his blue eyes tired as they skimmed past Brooke, without giving her a second glance, and rested on Carol.

'How are things?'

His voice was gentle and he sat down on the bed next to her as he leafed through the notes and traces that Brooke handed him.

'This all looks fine, Carol.'

'She's been moving around a lot and she's certainly made progress in the past few hours,' Brooke told him, her voice calm and professional. She concentrated hard on the notes—anything rather than look at the soft dark hair at the back of his neck. She knew how soft that hair felt, knew how every inch of him felt, and she loved him with every bone in her body—

'No pain relief at all?' Jed frowned and looked quizzically at Carol. 'You're fine about that, are you, Carol?'

'Brooke's helping me breathe and that helps a lot,' Carol said stoically. 'I really don't want anything else, Mr Matthews.'

Jed nodded slowly. 'OK, well, that's your decision, but let us know if you change your mind.'

'Is everything still all right?' Carol asked anxiously, and Jed nodded.

'At the moment everything seems fine but keep moving around. We do need to speed things up if we can. I'll pop back in another hour and examine you and we'll see where we go from there.'

Brooke watched him go, trying to ignore the pain in her chest. She couldn't carry on working in the unit and seeing him every day. It was torture. She was going to have to find another job, somewhere that put some distance between them. Life had to change.

CHAPTER TEN

Carol continued to make slow progress and by early evening she was ready to push.

'Is it nearly over?' She was clearly exhausted, her face pale and strained as she collapsed against the pillows after another contraction.

'You're doing so well, Carol. Just a little bit longer and then you're going to hold your baby.' Brooke brushed a strand of dark hair out her face, feeling almost exhausted as Carol. The responsibility for this particular delivery suddenly seemed enormous, and she checked the foetal heart again, reassuring herself that things were still going well.

An hour later the foetal heart was starting to cause her concern and Carol was clearly exhausted with the effort of trying to push.

Brooke pressed the buzzer and slipped an arm round Carol's shoulders. 'You're so tired, Carol. Take a few deep breaths. That's it. Well done.' She glanced up as Gill came into the room, her eyebrows raised. 'Could you bleep Jed for me, please?'

She could have done it herself, of course, but she didn't want to leave Carol even for a moment. They'd formed a bond during the long day and she knew that her presence was a comfort to the exhausted woman.

Gill gave a brief nod and left the room without a question, leaving Brooke to talk quietly to Carol.

'The baby isn't really moving down the birth canal any more,' Brooke said gently, 'and you seem so very tired that I wonder whether we should just ask Mr Matthews to fit a suction cap to the baby's head and give you a bit of extra help as you push.'

'Oh, I don't know.' Carol gave an exhausted sob and shook her head. 'I just don't know any more.'

The door opened and Jed strode in, his eyes immediately on Carol. 'How are you doing?'

'I'm not.' Carol shook her head. 'I can't do it.' Tears started to pour down her cheeks and Jed frowned and sat next to her, taking her hand in his.

'What do you mean, you can't do it? You nearly have done it, Carol. You've done brilliantly.' He turned to Brooke. 'Give me an update.'

She filled him in and he nodded quickly and turned back to Carol, his handsome face calm and reassuring. 'You're doing well, Carol. All we need to do now is help the baby down the last little bit.'

'Will it hurt him?' Carol wiped away the tears but still more fell and Brooke handed her a wad of tissues. 'I don't want to hurt him.'

Jed scanned the trace that Brooke handed him. 'The baby is getting tired now, Carol. We do need to deliver him. What I plan to do is use what we call the ventouse. It just means that next time you push I can help you by pulling the baby very gently. It won't hurt him and I promise I'll be very, very gentle.'

'What does Brooke think?' Carol looked trustingly at Brooke, who swallowed.

'I think you've been marvellous,' she said huskily. 'And this is going to be one lucky baby to have such a caring mum. But what he needs most of all right now is to be born, so why don't you let Mr Matthews help you?'

Carol nodded. 'OK, then. I trust you both. Will it hurt?'

Jed rolled up his sleeves and started to scrub while Brooke pressed the buzzer and got everything ready.

'Well, you've had no pain relief at all, so I'll use some local anaesthetic. I can't promise that it won't hurt at all but I'll be as gentle as I possibly can be.'

Quickly he and Brooke got everything ready and in an

amazingly short time Jed had managed to attach the cup to the head and was waiting for the next contraction.

'OK, big push for me now, Carol,' Jed said calmly, turning up the suction and pulling gently with the contraction. 'Good girl, that's brilliant.'

Carol flopped with tiredness between contractions and Brooke gave her some ice to suck.

'Nearly there, Carol.' She gave the woman a smile. 'Any minute now you're going to meet him—or her…'

'It's a him,' Carol murmured, her eyes drifting shut. 'I just know it's a him. Oh, here we go again…'

She screwed up her face and Brooke watched while Jed used the suction, carefully guarding the perineum as the baby's head was born.

'Well done.' He carefully removed the cap and grinned at Carol. 'The head's delivered. One more contraction and we should be there.'

Brooke crossed her fingers as she stood ready to give an injection of Syntometrine, a drug which helped the uterus contract after delivery. Please, let there be no complications. Please…

There weren't, and the baby slithered out into Jed's hands. He immediately handed the squalling infant to his sobbing mother.

'Oh, Bill. Bill.' Carol couldn't stop crying and Brooke had to stop herself joining in. She couldn't look at Jed, who was now clamping the cord and delivering the placenta.

Sita popped her head round the door and grinned delightedly. 'No one needs me, then?'

Jed shook his head. 'Everything's just fine. She's our star mum.'

Carol reached out a hand to Brooke. 'I can't thank you enough. You were so brilliant. Isn't she the best, Mr Matthews?'

'Definitely.' Jed gave a crooked smile and ripped off his gloves. 'She definitely is the best. Congratulations, Carol.'

And with that he turned on his heel and left the room, the door swinging shut behind him.

By the time Brooke had collected Toby and driven to the cottage, she was exhausted. Fortunately Toby was also tired after his exciting night with his friend and seemed sleepy in the car. Until he realised that they weren't going back to Jed's.

'Why aren't we going there?'

Brooke gritted her teeth. 'Because this is our home, darling.'

'But I liked living with Jed,' Toby grumbled, his bottom lip sticking out in a pout as he stared out of the car window. 'I want to carry on living with Jed.'

'Well, we can't,' Brooke said quietly, pulling up outside the cottage with a frown. She was expecting to see a tarpaulin over the roof but there was nothing, and it seemed as though the missing tiles had been replaced. Who had authorised that? She certainly hadn't spoken to anyone. She'd been so busy all week she hadn't even had time to call the insurance company.

Still frowning, she unlocked the front door and stared anxiously into the hall, wondering what state the soaked carpet was now in.

'Why have we got a new carpet?' Toby stared at the carpet and then at his mother who was slowly starting to simmer. Toby was right. The carpet was new. This must be Jed's handiwork again. She tilted her head and, sure enough, the ceiling had been repainted and there was no sign of the water stain.

Upstairs was now immaculate. Toby's bedroom had been completely redecorated and was cosy and snug.

'Wow! I can go back in my room!' Toby danced with delight and Brooke forced herself to unpack the bags and settle themselves back into the cottage again.

Once Toby was asleep she wandered down to her tiny living room and flopped onto one of the sofas.

Why had Jed done it? Why hadn't he asked her first? It

was like the car. He just took over and made these huge financial gestures to appease his conscience. Well, first thing tomorrow when he came to pick up Toby she was going to give him a piece of her mind.

He arrived just after eight the next morning, freshly shaved and wearing a pair of snug jeans and a dark-coloured sweatshirt which emphasised the width of his shoulders.

'Is he ready?'

No polite greetings or warmth, just straight to the point. He wanted Toby.

'Why didn't you tell me?' She glared at him and stroked her dark hair away from her face with a shaking hand. 'Why didn't you tell me, Jed?'

'Why didn't I tell you what?' His blue eyes were glacial and she felt her heart beat faster.

'I assumed that when you contacted the roofer, it was just an emergency measure. I didn't realise that you were planning a complete refit.'

His jaw hardened. 'You're telling me you wanted your cottage left like that?'

Brooke glared at him, her eyes hurt. Did he really not understand why she was upset? 'No, of course not. But I can manage by myself. You don't need to keep stepping in. First the car and now this. How many times do I have to tell you that you don't owe me anything?'

'It's nothing to do with owing you anything.' His words were clipped and his eyes were suddenly tired. 'I just thought—' He broke off and let out an impatient sigh, shaking his head in disbelief.

'What did you think Jed?'

'I thought you'd be pleased,' he said finally, dragging long fingers through his dark hair. 'You were so upset about it last week that I contacted your insurance company, got the quotes and had the work done.'

'I could have sorted out the insurance company myself,' Brooke said hoarsely, and he nodded.

'Well, I know that. I never once thought you weren't able

to do it. I just thought you might prefer to have some help. It's the sort of thing that families do in a crisis. They help each other out. Phil did the plastering and Tom and Dad did the painting.'

Brooke licked dry lips. 'Your family did it?'

His family had done all that? For her?

'That's right.'

'And the carpet?' Brooke muttered. 'What about that?'

'It's a small hallway, Brooke.' He rubbed the back of his neck and looked exasperated. 'Phil had a piece of carpet left over from one of the properties he lets. He used that. It was no big deal.'

Why had they gone to so much trouble for her?

Her head started to throb. 'They didn't need to do all that for me. I could have done it myself.'

'None of us doubted that.' A muscle worked in his lean jaw and he watched her for a moment, his blue eyes sweeping every inch of her face. 'If you're expecting me to apologise for helping you out, you're going to wait a long time. It wasn't because we didn't think you could do it yourself. It's just that we thought it would be a nice surprise if we did it for you. That's what family is for. It's about pulling together.'

Brooke looked away, her face flushed. Hadn't she said almost exactly the same thing to Mrs Baxter when she'd torn her off a strip for not standing by her daughter? The trouble was, she didn't know the first thing about pulling together. Her family had never been like that.

'I'm not part of your family, Jed,' she mumbled, and he stared at her, his gaze unflinching.

'You could be. We all want you to be. My mum and dad adore you. Tom thinks you're the answer to all men's dreams, and even the animals think you're worth licking. Phil thinks you're worth rearranging his entire work schedule for so that he can come and help you. But you think it's just because we all feel guilty and responsible for Toby. Don't you, Brooke?'

She didn't know what she thought any more. 'I—I don't know, Jed, I—'

'Save it.' There were lines of tiredness round his blue eyes. 'We all want to draw you into the family but you've turned independence into an art form. You can't tell the difference between responsibility and love, and I've all but given up trying to show you the difference. Why do you really think I wanted to sort your cottage out for you?'

Brooke swallowed, barely able to find her voice. 'B-because of Toby?'

'No, Brooke.' He gave a tired smile and muttered something under his breath. 'It was nothing to do with Toby. I did it for you, because I love you. You were upset and you were struggling. I hated to see you struggle and I wanted to make life easier for you. It was nothing to do with Toby.'

She opened her mouth to speak again but he wouldn't be interrupted.

'Forget it, Brooke. There's no point in us having this discussion any more. I do have a sense of responsibility, that's true, but I can support Toby without involving myself with his mother.' He shook his head slowly. 'You're so determined to stay independent because you don't believe that I can love you for yourself, and the truth is I don't know how to convince you any more. I've shown you that I love you in every way I know, but it isn't enough, is it?'

Her heart was pounding uncomfortably. 'I'm still afraid you can't separate your feelings for me from your sense of responsibility—'

'Of course I can!' he exploded, raking a hand through his hair. 'What are you saying? That I'm pretending to be in love with you out of a sense of responsibility? Do you really think I'm that stupid? I do know what it takes to make a relationship work, Brooke. I've had a shining example under my nose for the best part of thirty-five years.'

Her knees were shaking so badly she could barely stand. 'I just can't believe you want me...'

'I know you can't, which brings us to an impasse.' He

gave a short laugh and a weary smile. 'Tom would see the funny side of this.'

'Is there one?' Brooke swallowed. She couldn't see a funny side. She'd never felt more confused in her life. Did he really love her? Did he really?

'Well, yes, there is, actually. If you've got a warped sense of humour like my younger brother.' There was a brief silence as he hesitated. 'It's hard to say this without sounding arrogant, and I certainly don't mean to, but do you have any idea how many women have wanted to hear me say I loved them?'

'Plenty, I should think,' Brooke said gruffly. It was part of the reason that she knew he couldn't love her. He could just about pick anyone he wanted.

'Well, there certainly have been a few,' he replied wryly, 'but shall I tell you something? They all waited in vain because I made up my mind when I was young that I would never, ever use that word unless I meant it. I never told a girl I loved her to get her into bed, I never lied and I never gave false hope to anyone. The truth is, I never used the word at all until I said it to you the other night, and you didn't want to hear it.'

Brooke's eyes widened and her breathing clogged in her throat. He'd never told anyone that he loved them? 'That can't be true.'

'Oh, it's true.' He gave a smile of self-mockery and glanced across her lawn towards the mountains. 'And now you understand why Tom would laugh. He would say it was poetic justice that I should at last understand what it's like to love someone who doesn't love you back.'

'Jed—'

'Of all the members of the fair sex that I could have fallen in love with, I had to pick a stubborn, mule-headed woman who doesn't trust me and never will. I must be a masochist. I accept that you don't love me, but we do need to establish some sort of relationship for Toby's sake. He has a family and a right to be a part of it, even if you don't love me enough to marry me and make it official.'

Brooke stared at him, her heart racing. He was asking her to marry him? He loved her? Really?

'That's all I wanted to say.' His eyes locked with hers, holding her captive. 'Come and pick up Toby at lunchtime. I'll have him ready.'

Brooke drove up the pitted lane towards the Matthews' farm, her hands trembling on the steering-wheel as she tried to hold it steady.

Jed loved her. He really loved her.

She believed him now. But was it too late?

She gave a groan of despair. Why hadn't she been able to trust him? Why? Would he listen to her now if she tried to explain, tried to tell him how she felt?

And had he really never said 'I love you' to anyone before her? No. He obviously hadn't. Jed was straight and honest and he would never use words that he didn't mean, she knew that now. But he'd said them to her.

And she had no doubt that he meant them.

She had no doubt now that he loved her.

She remembered how angry he'd been when he'd found out about Toby, but how quickly he'd controlled his emotions and insisted on listening to her point of view. She remembered all the things he'd done to try and make her life better, things she'd thought he was doing out of a sense of duty.

But it hadn't been duty. He'd been doing it because he cared for her, and all she'd been able to think of had been her own childhood, and how he must have been doing it out of a sense of responsibility.

But Jed did love her. Or at least he had until today. He'd said that he'd accepted that she didn't love him. So was that the end of it all? Or could she persuade him that she did love him? That she always had loved him?

She pulled up outside the farmhouse, staring at the

wooden tubs stuffed with daffodils and tulips. It was idyllic, the setting. In fact, everything about this family was idyllic. And she could be a part of it. Why had she hesitated?

'Hello, Brooke!' Ellie came to the door, a broad smile on her face and a bottle of champagne in her left hand. 'You're just in time. Phil's here with wonderful news.'

Brooke climbed out of her car and smoothed her soft floral skirt over the curve of her hips.

'I don't want to intrude,' she mumbled, but Ellie ignored her and swept her inside, her warmth like a balm to Brooke's emotions.

'Nonsense! You're one of the family! How could you possibly intrude? You must join us for our celebration. Even Toby has a glass of lemonade!' She sailed into the kitchen with Brooke behind her. 'It's Brooke, everyone! Someone pour the girl a glass of champers.'

Before she knew what was happening a narrow champagne flute was thrust into her hand and she was drinking the health of Phil and his girlfriend who had just become engaged. Jed raised his glass with the rest of them, his smile ever present but his blue eyes strained and tired.

Brooke felt her insides turn over. She needed to talk to him. She needed to tell him that she loved him before it was too late. But how could she when they were surrounded by all these people?

'What's engaged?' Toby piped up, his little voice cutting through the excited buzz of conversation round the table.

'It's what you do before you get married,' Ellie told him with a broad smile. 'Phil and Rosie love each other, so they're getting married.'

Toby looked puzzled. 'But you don't get married just because you love each other.'

Ellie gave him a tolerant smile. 'Well, you do usually, dear.'

Toby shook his head violently. 'No. That's not right. My mum loved my dad and they didn't get married.'

There was a hideous silence and Brooke felt her breathing

stop as everyone turned to look at her. All except Jed, that was. He was staring at Toby.

'What did you say, old son?' His voice cracked slightly and he leaned forward and looked at Toby intently.

'My mum loved my dad. And they didn't get married.'

Brooke intervened, her voice strangled. This wasn't what she'd had in mind. 'Jed...'

Jed ignored her. 'What do you know about your dad, Toby?'

Toby swung his legs and tilted his head to one side, oblivious of the fact that you could have heard a pin drop in the room. 'I know my mum loved him more than any man in the whole world. She told me that. And because she couldn't marry him, she won't marry anyone. Ever. And that's why she's not married. She told me that, too.'

The silence seemed to last for ages and then Tom, uncharacteristically tactful, cleared his throat.

'Perhaps we should go and see the lambs—'

'No!' Jed stood up abruptly, his chair scraping on the kitchen floor. 'Mum, keep Toby company, will you? Brooke and I are going for a walk.'

Her knees shaking, Brooke stood up, unable to see how she could argue. Judging from the set look on his face, if she didn't go with him he'd have the conversation right here and now in front of his family, regardless of the audience.

'Excuse us, everyone.' His hand closed like a vice around her wrist and he led her into the yard and towards the stream she'd sat by on the first day he'd brought her to meet his parents.

Once there he released her and took a deep breath, his blue eyes watchful. 'OK, Brooke. What was that all about?'

Brooke took a deep breath. 'Toby knows I love his father and that I always will.'

Jed's breathing was uneven, his expression guarded. 'You told him that you loved me?'

'That's right.' She nodded slowly and he grasped her arms and stared intently into her dark eyes.

'When did you tell him that, Brooke?'

Her heart was thumping in her chest. 'He's always known. Ever since he was old enough to talk about it.'

Jed's hands tightened on her arms. 'You're telling me that you loved me from the beginning?'

'I could never love anyone else,' she said simply, a lump building in her throat as he closed his eyes. Was she too late?

Jed blinked and shook his head as if to clear it. 'But you had other relationships...'

She looked away. 'There weren't any other relationships, Jed.'

'There weren't?' His voice was hoarse. 'But you let me think— Why?'

Her smile was wry and she scuffed the soft earth with the toe of her boot. 'You're a clever man. You work it out.'

There was a brief silence while his eyes searched hers. 'Because had I known that you hadn't had another relationship with anyone after that night with me, I would have put two and two together,' he said gruffly, 'and I would have come to the conclusion that that night we spent together meant as much to you as it did to me. Am I right?'

Brooke felt his hands turn her to face him and she closed her eyes.

'Am I right, Brooke? Dammit, look at me!'

She responded to his rough command and the look in his eyes made her nerves tingle and her insides tumble.

He shook his head in disbelief. 'You're saying that you loved me from the beginning, but you didn't tell me because you were convinced I couldn't possibly feel the same way about you and that I would marry you out of a sense of responsibility. Is that right?'

Brooke nodded and he gave a low growl and pulled her against him.

'You crazy, stubborn woman!' His hands cupped her face and his eyes held hers. 'I felt the same way as you. I loved you from that first night, impossible though it seemed. I was desperate to find you—you have no idea how desperate. And then when I failed I thought I'd go mad.'

'Jed...' His words made her heartbeat quicken and he lifted her hand and kissed the tips of her fingers.

'And then when I did find you, you fought me all the way. That night we made love, I told you I loved you then— so why did you run?'

'I didn't believe you,' she mumbled, her cheeks pink as she recalled how stupid she'd been.

He looked puzzled. 'But why would I lie?'

'Because—' she broke off, thoroughly embarrassed. 'Oh, for goodness' sake, Jed! Men say all sorts of things they don't mean when they're in that position.'

'What, making love, you mean?' He grinned down at her, his elation evident. 'Well, you wouldn't exactly know that, would you, my sweet? Seeing as I'm the only man that's had that privilege. And I can assure you for the record that I never say anything I don't mean, even when I'm at my most vulnerable.'

'And you only said it once,' Brooke said gruffly, her eyes shy as they met the warmth in his.

'Because you didn't say it back and I was afraid I'd scare you off,' he murmured, pulling her into his arms. 'And you still haven't told me why you ran the next morning.'

Brooke bit her lip. 'I overheard Tom telling you that you had to get married. That you didn't have any choice.'

Jed stared at her, his blue eyes narrowed as he tried to recall the conversation. His brow cleared and he nodded slowly. 'You're right, he did say that, but what he meant was that I'd be crazy to let you go because I loved you so much. Tom is one of the few people who knows how I feel about you. He was afraid that I'd spent so long avoiding marriage that I'd let you slip through my fingers. It wasn't anything to do with Toby. In fact, Tom doesn't know about Toby. I only told Mum and Dad and they're sworn to secrecy until we work out what we're going to do. Tom was just giving me some brotherly advice.'

Brooke's eyes widened and a soft smile touched her mouth. 'And are you going to follow his advice, Jed?'

'Definitely.' He grinned. 'For once my little brother is talking sense. You're going to marry me, Brooke Daniels. You're going to put me out of my misery and say yes.'

A bubble of pure happiness rose inside her and she touched his rough cheek with shaking fingers. 'I can't believe this is happening.'

'Believe it,' he growled, turning his face to kiss her fingers. 'I always knew we'd be together in the end.'

'I didn't,' she confessed, her cheeks heating slightly at the look in his eyes. Jed was an incredibly sexy man. 'It was what I wanted, I knew that from the very first, but every time I managed to persuade myself that it might work, that you might really want me for myself, I remembered my father. I just couldn't bring myself to trust you in case you hurt Toby. And me.'

'Understand something, Brooke.' His voice shook with sincerity. 'I would never, *ever* do anything to hurt you or our child. Do you believe me? Do you?'

She gave a nod, her small hands tangling in the front of his shirt. 'I do believe you. I should have trusted you all along, but I didn't dare. I just kept remembering my father. And I was so stubborn—'

'No!' Jed's eyes danced. 'Were you? I hadn't noticed.'

She smiled shyly. 'I must have seemed so ungrateful—all those things you did for me and I kept accusing you of acting out of a sense of responsibility.'

'You weren't ungrateful,' he said softly, 'just very badly hurt in the past. But that's where it stays, Brooke. In the past. I'm not your father and I'm nothing like him.'

Her eyes locked with his. 'I know that, Jed.'

'I love you, sweetheart.' His voice was deep and very, very male. 'Not because of Toby, but because of you. If Toby had never happened I would still love you.'

'Oh, Jed.' Her eyes filled and she stood on tiptoe to kiss his cheek. 'I love you, too—so very much.'

His hands cupped her face. 'So is that a yes? Will you marry me?'

Ecstatically happy, her eyes teased him. 'I don't remember you proposing.'

Jed glanced down at the muddy ground, a rueful expression on his handsome face. 'You want me on one knee? It's been raining all day—I'll ruin my trousers.'

She giggled. 'Wimp! Oh, well, I suppose I'll have to make do.'

'Make do?' He swept her into his arms, his face only inches from hers, his blue eyes alight with laughter. 'You're a demanding woman, do you know that? Will you marry me, Brooke?'

'Yes.' Her voice was little more than a whisper. 'Yes, yes yes.'

He lowered his head, his kiss a gentle demonstration of all the love that he felt, and she returned the kiss with everything that was in her heart.

'Come on.' He lifted his head, a triumphant smile playing around his firm mouth. 'There's champagne on offer inside. We deserve it.'

Lowering her to the ground, he slipped an arm round her shoulders as they walked back to the farmhouse. Jed opened the door, grinning broadly at his entire family as they watched him with a mixture of speculation and trepidation.

'Mum, can you send Toby out here, please?' Jed pulled Brooke into his arms and kissed her gently in front of his smiling family. 'We've got something to tell him.'

MILLS & BOON®

Makes any time special™

Mills & Boon publish 29 new titles every month. Select from...

Modern Romance™   Tender Romance™

Sensual Romance™

Medical Romance™   Historical Romance™

MILLS & BOON

Medical Romance™

CLAIMED: ONE WIFE by Meredith Webber
Book two of The Australian Doctors duo

Neurosurgeon Grant Hudson knows that fraternisation between colleagues can break hearts, ruin careers and even lives. Yet for Dr Sally Cochrane, he is prepared to break his own rule. Sally, however, has her own reasons for keeping him out of her life…

A NURSE'S FORGIVENESS by Jessica Matthews
Book one of Nurses Who Dare trilogy

Marta Wyman is not going to let Dr Evan Gallagher pressurise her into meeting up with her grandfather. No matter how handsome, polite and charming Evan is he will have a long wait before she changes her mind—or gives in to her desires…

THE ITALIAN DOCTOR by Jennifer Taylor
Dalverston General Hospital

Resentment simmered between Luke Fabrizzi and Maggie Carr when her family tried to introduce them with marriage in mind. But a staged relationship in order to avert their families led to a truce—and another battle against their true feelings!

On sale 4th May 2001

Available at most branches of WH Smith, Tesco, Martins, Borders, Easons, Volume One/James Thin and most good paperback bookshops

MILLS & BOON

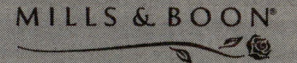

Medical Romance™

NURSE IN NEED by *Alison Roberts*

Emergency nurse Amy Brooks rushed into an engagement when she realised she wanted a family of her own—then she met Dr Tom Barlow. She had to end the engagement and Tom was delighted—but was his love for Amy the real reason?

THE GENTLE TOUCH by *Margaret O'Neill*

Jeremy is asked to persuade Veronica Lord into letting him treat her. Just as he gains her trust, Jeremy discovers that he was present when she had her accident and could have helped her. Will she ever be able to forgive him, let alone love him?

SAVING SUZANNAH by *Abigail Gordon*

Until Dr Lafe Hilliard found her, Suzannah Scott believed she had nothing left. Lafe helped her to rebuild her life and all he wanted in return was honesty. But if Suzannah revealed her past, she risked not only losing his professional respect, but his love...

On sale 4th May 2001

Available at most branches of WH Smith, Tesco, Martins, Borders, Easons, Volume One/James Thin and most good paperback bookshops

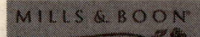

MILLS & BOON

DAKOTA BORN

Debbie Macomber
NEW YORK TIMES BESTSELLING AUTHOR

Lindsay's looking for a fresh start—and Dakota holds the key to her past, and a secret she's determined to uncover...

Published 20th April

MILLS & BOON

STEEP/RTL/1

The STEEPWOOD Scandal

REGENCY DRAMA, INTRIGUE, MISCHIEF... AND MARRIAGE

A new collection of 16 linked
Regency Romances, set in the villages
surrounding Steepwood Abbey.

Book 1
Lord Ravensden's Marriage
by Anne Herries

Available 4th May

*Available at branches of WH Smith, Tesco,
Martins, RS McCall, Forbuoys, Borders, Easons,
Volume One/James Thin and most good paperback bookshops*